NNÉNNA

Appreciated

[signature]
1/4/13

OTHER NOVELS BY THE AUTHOR
Jaundiced Justice
Blighted Blues

NNÉNNA
My Daughter, My Mother

A Novel by
M. O. Ené

Reedbuck, Inc.
Everything else is embellishment.

Published by:
   Reedbuck, Inc.
   P. O. Box 150
   Bloomfield, NJ 07003
   USA
   reedbuck@aol.com

© M. O. Ené, December 7, 2007

ISBN 1-4348-9263-8

All locations and names are fictional. The names of recognizable real persons, real events, and real places convey only a sense of verisimilitude.

All rights reserved.
Do not reproduce, store in a retrieval system, or transmit any part of this book at any time or by any means without the prior permission of the publisher.

Ịfụnanya

Printed and bound in the
United States of America

Love is a passing psychosis, a phase of deep psychological distraction, or a momentary mental mess of varying duration. Since all stages in sanity-insanity spectrum affect different people differently, different people react to love lunacy differently.

Cover Concept:
Peter A. Maduabum, Esq.

Prologue

THERE IS NO IOTA OF DOUBT IN GILBERT'S MIND; the bouncing baby, his first child, is the reincarnation of his beloved mother. He was expecting her. On the night his mother passed away, four months earlier, she promised to see him soon. The gorgeous girl's arrival was soon enough. He knew at once because he felt it. He liked and loved what he saw. Gilbert named her, Nnénnaya, meaning 'mother of her father.'

The notion of reincarnation is profound, yet in Igbo theosophy, it does not quite capture the complex but credible concept of 'coming back'—to *reflesh*... to make flesh again. Coming back to life is actually more spiritual than physical because every child is a returning replica of a dear departed or, often, a living nearest and dearest. If anyone reincarnates in reality, it is *ọgbanje*: the stubborn spirit child—usually beautiful and female—who has links to two worlds, willfully going and coming. The cursed child dies and returns to torment the same mother until stopped by ritually cutting the inter-realm bond, freeing her to live here or in netherworld.

Nnénna is not *ọgbanje*; she is the symbolic and spiritual return of her daddy's dear departed mother—her *ịnọụwa*.

Over twenty years later, the arrival of Nnénna remains an historic milestone in Eziuke and many communities beyond, a reference point for children born around January 15, 1970: Nigeria's post-Biafran babies.

The other day, in the marketplace, a palm-oil retailer faulted her daughter's endless financial demands, which were straining her matrimonial peace. Her petty trading venture was to help her husband in the struggle to educate their daughter beyond high school.

"Was she not born before Nnénna, the girl-child of Gilbert Iké?" a stall mate asked her, knowingly.

"Of course," she responded nonetheless. "Many moons and several sunrises before China—that's Nnénna's mother—stopped jumping in and out of different flashy cars, that girl of mine was already sucking my two breasts flat out. By the time Nnénna arrived, my blockhead of a daft daughter had sentenced me to a long life of padded *koloshéeti*." She paused to show her bleached brassiere—a bedraggled and baggy secondhand undergarment—to drive home her point.

"Then she should be in a man's house now. The teacher training college she is attending takes time and too much money," her mate asserted matter-of-factly.

"And it is only elementary school teacher. Tell me, how much does the government pay teachers? What is Nnénna, eh? She is a lawyer and a big company chief. I hear that the helicopter that flies past before dusk on Eke market days brings her and her many assistants in Lagos back to Enugu."

Apparently, no one told her how Nnénna and supposedly numerous assistants fit into a noisy helicopter every fourth morning and make it to Lagos before dawn.

Different people say different things about Gilbert's only child, exaggerated or not. Some are sincere admirations and respect for stainless success; others are easily execrable envy and jaded jealousy. In sixteen years of existence and living—and what a life—Nnénna never asked for a penny. The need never arose. The first time she touched money, any currency, was to pay a London taxi fare.

This is the magic of Nnénna. She was born under a super-stellar constellation, a bright and big star that comes once in seventy age grades. She was born with silver streaks gracing her golden glitter. Forget that she was running before her mates learnt to crawl, Nnénna Iké epitomizes a rarity in her cultural setting because she was born all over again to live life again and to live it abundantly.

1

GILBERT IS AN EVERYDAY SUCCESS STORY IN the many cultured communities east of the Niger. After secondary education, he sat for his A-Level examinations from home. He passed the three enrolled subjects with good grades and got a job with the regional ministry of agriculture as a purchasing officer. He took care of his mother and saved for his university education.

Four years later, precisely on January 15, 1966, the military struck and dismantled the First Republic. The coup d'état begot another coup and a pogrom. Those who supposedly knew better decided in a moment of madness to resort to matured mayhem: War broke out.

His mapped-out move to tertiary academic activities stalled. He enlisted in the secessionist army as an officer, determined to make sure that the invaders did not get near his mother in Eziuke. The Federal troops soon sacked Enugu, the capital city, and surrounding suburbia. The military authorities redeployed him to a battlefront far from his hometown. His mother moved with the refugee bandwagons when Eziuke fell to the Federal soldiers. She went through hell alone, moving from one refugee camp to another in breakaway Republic of Biafra.

Lt. Gilbert Iké sought her whereabouts. Sources told him she was at a refugee camp in Awgu. He arranged to meet with her at the town's main market. His superior denied his release request. He went AWOL. It was a risk he could live with; losing his mother to the war, he might not outlive. Unfortunately, they did not meet until the fomented fratricide stopped in 1970.

He feared that she had died in the infamous Awgu market air-raid massacre, which took place on the day they were supposed to meet there. She feared that he could not make it because he had fallen at a battlefront. Life is not worth living if life itself snuffs out in its prime. Gilbert Iké was her life, her only son and her only issue. She lived for him, and his world revolved around her.

Her elder brother, Chief Chimaobim Chimé, who was the chief of the neighboring town of Umuchimé, heard of her plight. He paid smugglers to bring her back to their district, now in the occupied or liberated territory called Biafra II or East Central State of Nigeria respectively—depending on the radio station to which one listened.

Gilbert moved back to his unit after serving detention in a guardroom at 52 Division HQ for desertion. At this point, he was tempted to quit the struggle, but there was no legitimate option for grown Biafran males. The war was everything.

Rather than run to live in Nigeria, Gilbert chose to fight and die a Biafran in Biafra. The next war operation was his last: an elite federal sniper shot and nearly killed him. The sniper had killed three Biafran officers in the heat of a bloody battle before his luck ran out. Bleeding but able to function, he located the sniper's position and brought him down with a clean shot that missed his groin by inches. Both men looked at each other. They were both bleeding. Hurting, humbled, and hardly holding up hope, they shook hands and helped each other to their feet. Gilbert looked at him intensely and felt like slapping him.

"Captain Yerima Sambo-Razaq, Nigerian Army."

"Lieutenant Gilbert Chimaobim Iké, Biafran Army."

With the officious introduction, they limped away in opposite directions. Gilbert had no regrets at all because, to him, no one has the right to take a human life.

Gilbert was at a makeshift hospital for 10 weeks. The determination to find out what happened to his mother kept him going. With a funny limp and unable to go back to active service, he got his late promotion to captain. He was made an army supply-and-transport (S&T) officer.

*

After the war, Gilbert came back home to Eziuke. His mother was alive. She told him she had left Biafra and returned home to die in peace. She did not die. People at home were living a relatively decent life, farming and tending their livestock. He swore never to leave her again.

Gilbert gave up further academic pursuit and, like many Igbo youths of the postwar era, he chose commerce. He went into commodity supply. A contractor of sorts, he supplied whatever people wanted. He operated from Eziuke—about 20 miles outside Enugu—though opening early and closing late could have maximized his profit margin. Money is not everything; his mother was his life.

As with many one-man operators, making ends meet was an uphill hike. Gilbert was an ambitious young man. He was determined to provide his mother with possible, postwar modern comforts. Having made many useful contacts during the war, he linked them into an effective network of clients, suppliers, providers, and friends.

Mighty Giles International Ltd boomed. He prospered, despite several strangulating postwar policies of Nigerian government, which weighed down the apparent losers in a polity that proclaimed 'no victor, no vanquished.'

Mother and son were very close, so close that no other woman meant much to him. He was 25, and he was not dating. His mates who did not come home with wives were getting married. Every weekend was a wedding weekend, but nothing moved Gilbert to consider the available bevy of beauties in Eziuke and in Enugu.

Christmas morning, 1970, Gilbert's mother became too ill, a direct result of the irreversible ravages of war. The brief date with kwashiorkor had taken its toll. She knew there was nothing medical science could do for her and that she was becoming a hindrance rather than the huge help her son needed.

Everybody looked forward to celebrating the first Christmas after the civil war as civilized as it ought to be. Mrs. Obiagæli Iké put up a brave face for the holiday. By sundown, she sat her son down and bluntly requested to see a grandchild before she moved over to submit her books, an idiomatic expression that means meeting her maker. She told Gilbert that the local beauties sashaying around had lifelong policies and pro-community plans he could help them to accomplish.

"In every market, there are buyers and there are also sellers. You make inquiries, you haggle, and you look for best bargains. Listen: All the makeup these women wear on Sundays is not for fun. You understand?"

"Mama, we don't need a wonder woman to make our lives difficult," Gilbert protested. "I don't want a woman to come between us, some living fire that will burn the thread that holds us together. Mama, it is not worth it."

"My son," she said as if she was talking to a toddler. "Men marry wives, not their mothers."

"Maybe in Greek mythology," Gilbert mumbled.

"I don't know why you are mumbling, but this is no time to exhibit hard-headedness."

He was obviously making light of the discussion by recalling the legend of Prince Oedipus, who killed his father, then married and fathered children with his mother. In the Greek legend, the parents tried to avoid the obvious fluke of fate. Inadvertently, they fulfilled the far-fetched prophecy.

Probably, he thought, the Greeks could have avoided the horrible outcomes had they dealt with the realities of the matter; a postponed problem produces problems.

In Igbo mythology, such an abominable liaison is so unthinkable no one tries to explain it. However, Oedipus complex as proposed by Jewish psychoanalyst Sigmund Freud is not a strange concept. A son's affection for his mother is stronger than his respect for the father. Nothing else underlines the concept more than the intense reaction of Igbo male teenagers to the apparently naive expression, '*nné gi*' (your mother); '*nna*' (father) sounds bland.

"I don't know why you are smiling. This is a serious matter. What do I tell the Big Man up there that I achieved on earth? 'Wait until my son comes in,' eh? Believe me, I know how you feel, but think about it: If we go through another murderous madness, like the hell-on-earth we just came out from, nobody will know we ever existed."

She was right; he knew it. He was smiling because he recalled the first time he beat up a chap for saying '*Waka*' with the five fingers of both hands bared at him. The term —from '*uwa ka*' (Hausa phrase for 'your mother')—was considered very offensive and deeply disgusting. Solving the matter later, his uncle Chimé faulted him: "You did not allow the poor boy to finish his statement. He could be saying that your mother has lucky hands… *akanchawa*, or that she is as beautiful as his clean palms."

Gilbert adored his mother, and he was not against the marriage institution. The other day in the capital city's main market, he explained to a friend that he focused more on his mother and his business, not that he feared to marry. Then again, the fear of marriage is real in men his age. The society is so pushy in pairing up men and women it often forgets the hard work involved in making the magic of matrimony.

It is indeed a miracle that two total strangers meet, fall in love, and live together until death do them part. It is scary in parts, but it is indeed a natural wonder. It is sheer good luck that couples find each other at the right time, at the right place, and live together for as long as it lasts. There must be something much more than love that explains the sustenance of this wonder of the world.

Gilbert thought about the chances of getting the right woman at the right time: There is no formula for knowing who will refuse to let go when you no longer want her, or who will go when you truly want her to stay. Divorce is not the norm, but it is not a taboo.

Chief Chimé once told Gilbert to leave the decision to destiny: "A wife is like packaged merchandise introduced newly to the market," he counseled while they shared a gallon of palm wine at the Chimé Estate in Umuchimé. "You cannot trust the label to give an accurate description of the content. You buy it on trust, just as we bought this wine on trust; whatever you see inside is what you get."

"Trust?" Gilbert queried.

"Yes, trust. Listen to me: Love, good cooking, great bedmate, and all the fancy stuff that hopeless romantics regard as ingredients of good marriage are fantasy."

Gilbert thought about the underlying philosophy of marriage, but he was often too busy to devote time to its knots and nuances. He was a very busy man. Besides prospering in supply business, he bought bombed-out buildings in the city and renovated them. He recently bought and rebuilt two burnt bungalows and rented one to an officer of the victorious army, the same officer who almost killed him, whose life he had spared only months before: now Major Yerima Sambo-Razaq.

2

GILBERT GOT A WIFE; NO, HIS MOTHER CHOSE one: a very beautiful girl who was heading for the spinster shelf because she looked too *imported* and behaved badly. Chināsa Ezenāgu was in a class all her own. She was nicknamed 'China' because her skin tone was more like the delicious and sparkling palm oil from Akægbe, a hardworking community just south of Enugu, the Coal City —it was not a short form of her name. As if having physical features that stood her out was not enough, Chināsa was born out of wedlock by a rebellious youth.

After the elder Ezenāgu girls had left home, her mother stayed back to provide an heir. Chināsa came instead. Pa Ezenāgu went for a second wife, a preposition he had kicked against because he was trying to be a good Catholic, instead of a normal Anglican he was. Within months, the new wife had a baby boy. Actually, she had come with the child. This was the key component that made the huge age difference irrelevant in the managed-marriage contract.

Chināsa's mother, Abigail Ezenāgu, gave up the fight for family lineage as soon as the seventeen-year-old girl settled in as the new wife of her seventy-year-old frail father. Abigail married *Alhaji* Abbas Madaki, a wealthy Muslim magnate who wanted an heir. She succeeded.

Chināsa was pretty, and she flaunted it. She grew up in comfort, thanks to her stepfather. Though he loved her like his own daughter, she refused to compromise her Christian values for his Islamic faith. Nonetheless, Madaki sent her to good Christian schools in then Eastern Region, and she lacked nothing that money could buy.

During the civil war, to avoid unforeseen unpleasantness emanating from fanatical ethnic cleansing sweeping across Northern and Western Regions, Madaki sent Abigail and Chināsa to London. The boy that Abigail had for Madaki was already at Barewa College, Zaria, also called 'Eton of the North.' His mother's ethnic extraction was not detrimental in Nigeria's volatile inter-ethnic hostilities because many ethnic nations are patrilineal. With his third wife, Abigail, and stepdaughter out of the way, Madaki took a fourth wife.

Chināsa came back to Enugu soon after the staged truce of January 15, 1970. She was liberated and too liberal for then East Central State. Men came rushing in from everywhere like moths to light. The local boys could not compete for her affection. She was beautiful, articulate, intelligent, and a swinging sixties chick, but she was naive. Many men still thrived in the decadence of the war era. Hit-and-run hustlers were many, and they scored whenever they went out to play. They had the time and the money, and they played mostly away. It was okay for them to bed her, but they never took her home to their parents, or to their madams in many cases.

The stories fabricated about Chināsa by village rumor mills churned decent stomachs. Some said that a sea creature had walked about as a man, met her mother Abigail, who was the village tart, and impregnated her. Others claimed that they had looked backwards through their legs and had seen that her two feet did not make contact with the ground. One loafer swore that bending to look backwards through the legs was not necessary: Her feet did not touch the ground at Eke Eziuke, the local market notorious for its dog stalls. Of course, 'her feet did not touch the ground'—she wore high-heeled shoes. These and other malicious myths generally stuck because there was no strong, local male figure to stand up for her. Chināsa was a lost soul.

Enter Gilbert's mother.

Gilbert's mother knew about the Ezenāgu family history. Chināsa's biological father was not local. Of part-African and part-European ancestry, Mr. Fynecountry was a senior civil servant of Niger Delta origin. A wild teenager, Abigail ended up in his bed. Married with grown children, the colonial civil servant covered his tracks by taking an early retirement and moving back to his native island of Bonny.

Mr. Fynecountry should not have bothered: Abigail was free to procreate to guarantee the Ezenāgu genealogy. It was not unprecedented; in fact, it was the custom in parts of the Igbo nation. The first daughter in a family without a male offspring assured continuity of the lineage. She could marry out thereafter, if she so desired, or she could stay back and enjoy the complete and combined privileges of a kindred's daughter and wife. Pa Ezenāgu had embraced Christianity. He did not press the issue before his older daughters married.

Chināsa came back to Eziuke long before 1970 Christmas to recover from a near-disastrous, quack abortion. Her fair-weather friends deserted her. Her mother, Abigail, was still in London. Her grandfather had died before the war. His young widow and her children, including those that came after the man had passed, did not want her around. Because of her lifestyle, aunts and cousins stayed aloof. In some societies, she could have killed herself, but not in Eziuke. Suicide is *alụ*, abomination. Eziuke buried suicides like putrefied garbage.

Madaki loved his stepdaughter, but he demanded a little decorum and an observance of basic societal rules that were not necessarily Islamic. He considered it very disrespectful that she flew back home alone from Britain soon after the cessation of hostilities and before his say-so.

Gilbert's mother Obiagæli was poor in health, but she felt for Chināsa. Often, she cooked for Chināsa and, sometimes, she walked over to her village and nursed her. She knew how callous their society could be. She was a living example.

Chināsa became the daughter she had dreamt of having after producing the almost obligatory male. When she observed that Chināsa was having problems communicating with her, and on confirming what she had suspected, she told Gilbert to contact any female friend closer to Chināsa's age.

That was how Gilbert got close to Chināsa. He traced and fetched Fanny, her girlfriend from high school. Biafra-weaned and street-smart, Fanny was another high flyer, but she knew the ropes and played safe, something no one taught Chināsa in London. They were birds of the same feather, but Chināsa flew too high into the air of sex revolution and crash-landed. Fanny took care of the intimate and intricate issues; Gilbert's mother provided the maternal anchor, to which they gravitated on weekends; and Gilbert supplied the dough that made the duo's do-nothing life livable. Gradually, Chināsa rose from her depression-induced breakdown.

Gilbert trusted his mother's judgment and proposed to Chināsa. Eminent emissaries emerged from all nooks and crannies of the extended family to give unsolicited advice. His uncle, the only person who had a moral right to object, did not. The more opposing views Gilbert got from folks, the more determined he was to marry Chināsa. People said that Obiagæli was digging her only son's grave.

"That's why her husband died as soon as he married her. She wants to do the same to her son—her own flesh and blood," a notorious local loudmouth babbled.

"The children of *Nze* Chimé are too assertive for their own good," her gossip-gang mate replied.

"Somebody must stop her before it is too late."

Before walking away, the snoopy duo reenacted the ritual of personal purification. Almost at the same rate, the women whirled their hands around their wrapped heads, snapped their fingers as far removed from their bodies as possible, and said in unison, *"Tụfiakwa!"*

It was hard to understand what they exorcised: the audio-offensiveness of their verbal diarrhea, the vain vulgarity of sticking their dirty fingers into other people's pretty pot of porridge, or the assumed atrocities of the descendants of the late prominent paramount chief of Umuchimé.

"The fun-filled fast lanes of life often lead to unmitigated misery in the paradise of fools," an old village headmaster cautioned at the local watering hole up the dusty road.

"He who is refused smoked fish says it is bitter anyway," a known freeloader wisecracked.

"Hear the village idiot!"

"Idiot or no idiot, Sir Retired-but-not-tired Headmaster, the head that drags the ear of this matter is that Gilbert has made his choice: China Ezenāgu is it. Is it too hard to accept that every man reserves the right to live his life as destined?"

"What do you know about destiny? Enjoy your free drink and just shut that mouth of a miserable miscreant!"

"Well, even if you buy all these drinks, I shall still speak my mind. Therefore, as I was saying, men of Eziuke should not be a part of female gossiping gangs."

"Did you all hear that?" The headmaster was now overly excited. "This is the sort of sordid statement that compels an Igbo person, any Igbo with complete dentition, to say, *Tụfịa*'! God forbid bad thing… abomination!"

"Are you calling us women?" another client at the bar queried pointedly, just to make sure he heard correctly.

"Are you men? You, Mr. Headmaster, are you a man?"

Before the village headmaster could chide the freeloader, the other client landed a swift left uppercut. The freeloader recovered rather quickly, picked up a half-empty big bottle of stout beer, knocked off the hard bottom to reveal jagged edges, and stood his ground. Everyone melted away from the bar, including the bartender. It took the intervention of more responsible citizens to bring the situation under control.

A marriage between two locals should have been a thing of joy but, to many local champions, the pairing did not seem right. To them, Chināsa contravened unwritten moral codes, the laws of the land, and still netted the most eligible bachelor in town.

'Good girls get good guys,' a good mother would tell her teenage daughter. 'Keep your legs apart and you will end up with a lousy lowborn loser.'

Many parents put it bluntly with such popular sayings as, 'If you conceive a child standing up, you will give birth to a psycho,' and 'eating without ample pecking causes instant death in fowls.' The idea is that no teenager should indulge in premarital sex, which is why no responsible elder tolerates goats in a yam barn, as in a boy and a girl staying home alone.

The Nigeria-Biafra War changed the Igbo society for the worst; Euro-colonial incursions had made it worse. The war simply completed the colonial contamination of the culture and the corruption of many traditional societies southeast of the River Niger. Chināsa brought home the truth: Girls can now keep their legs as wide apart as they want, for as long as they desire, and still net their God-given special spouses.

By netting Gilbert, a perfect partner, many townspeople reckoned that Chināsa was sending the wrong message to the youths of Eziuke. She showed that good girls do not always get good guys. Like the old village goat, she gnawed on a raw cassava tuber and lived to bleat about it.

Alas, it was too late for Eziuke townsfolk. At this point, it was like trying to read a pocket roadmap in rush-hour traffic. As her full Igbo name suitably suggests, *Chi na-asa okwu*— God responds more appropriately: a wise way of saying that the right response to mundane mumblings of mere mortals is not within the manipulations of men; it is divine-driven, and so was her meeting Gilbert.

3

GILBERT AND CHINĀSA WERE TO WED BEFORE the rage of rainy season returned with tropical fury. He had seen the person in Chināsa. He loved her like the sister he never had; she, like a full-blood brother. She had seen it all, and she was prepared to settle down and be a good girl and a wonderful wife. She was prepared to do any and everything possible to prove the green eyes of Eziuke wrong.

Since Gilbert lived mostly in his hometown, he scheduled the wedding to take place there. The traditional wedding ceremony was easy. Homefolks never expected Chināsa to amount to much; therefore, any gesture from Gilbert was extra. After the traditional rituals and just before the first proclamation of the banns, anonymous objections to the marriage reached the parish priest. It seemed that some people were determined not to allow Chināsa to get away easily with marrying the most eligible bachelor for as far as stories can travel.

The parish priest dismissed the petitions as the handwork of men of yesteryears. Father Charles O'Keeffe was a liberal, young Irish priest. He came to Africa to help with the Caritas relief operations in Biafra. He stayed back to teach Latin and theology at a local seminary before being lumbered with priestly duties. O'Keeffe enlivened churchgoing at Holy Family parish. His humanitarian roles during the bloody war endeared him to everyone, young and old, men and women, Christians and traditionalists. He was popular, especially with his surname supposedly sounding like that of the town's first colonial warrant chief, *Nze* Okechukwu Okéifè. O'Keeffe allowed the mispronunciation.

O'Keeffe was a bag of compromises. With his elastic policies, he opened up the mission to newcomers. He allowed dancing and the use of native musical instruments. A brief relapse into traditional beliefs was not fiercely condemned. The Roman Catholic Mission was rebuilding and seriously scavenging for new members in the face of rising Pentecostal and sundry spiritual churches. Fortunately, many Vatican policies did not contradict local norms. For example, teenage or premarital pregnancy was taboo. No sane soul talked of abortion. Homosexuality had no local name because it did not exist, presumably; local men grew up and married women. Male circumcision was compulsory at day seven.

O'Keeffe asked the church committee to discourage the spread of wicked rumors. He banned the acceptance of all anonymous petitions. When it became obvious that the same church committee members were orchestrating the scandal for an entirely different reason—Gilbert had not *seen* them—the priest was livid.

"Why should he *see* them?" he queried the catechist.

"Father, some suspect she is… a little pregnant."

"A little pregnant?" O'Keeffe laughed loudly. He had met Chināsa a few times since she started coming to Sunday services. He had heard all about her London sojourn, and her broadminded worldview impressed him. "Okay, Catechist, enough of this nonsense. Can't you see that the strain of rushed marriage ceremonies is too much, plus the church wedding preparations?"

"Father, it is true-o," the catechist countered sheepishly. His second son, a medical doctor, is O'Keeffe's age.

"Did your son treat her for 'a little pregnancy'?"

"Oh no, the women just know. You know, the signs and things: spitting, change in complexion, and other little, little things only women see easily."

"I see. You expect me to know such little, little things?"

The catechist had never thought about it. He had assumed that every adult should know. Thinking about it, he felt bad: The Irish priest was *fada*—a reverend father, not a biological father. He did not know whether to apologize or sympathize. His silence said it all.

"Well?" O'Keeffe persisted.

The catechist mumbled something, coughed to clear his head—not his throat, and then said, "No, Father."

O'Keeffe smiled and said, "Good. Do you mind telling those men and women to find something else to do, now that we both know that she is not 'a little pregnant'?"

"Yes, Father," he nodded—he would not mind.

The priest walked toward his parish mansion, which was more posh than the crumbling church. He was in no mood to perform his 'magical' acts for the children coming out from a catechism class. The most interesting magic was pulling out his teeth: He wore a set of false upper teeth, a direct result of a freak accident on a school camp holiday back in Ireland.

The children let him be. Only when he waved did they shout in unison: "*Gudu eveni', Fada!*"

Chināsa had actually taken in. She told the parish priest in her one and only confessional call. It was unplanned, and she did not think it was a *bad* sin. Besides, she and Gilbert were married according to the custom. "Do you, sir, recommend an abortion?" she asked O'Keeffe pointedly.

"Oh no, that is a serious sin; murder, if you ask me," he responded rather quickly. Case closed.

O'Keeffe knew it was the trend: Get a bride and score before taking her to the Lord; He will understand. Testing a product before buying reduces the queue at the refund counter: A childfree marriage was a surefire ground for all sorts of domestic discord and conjugal complications. In Chināsa's case, she initiated it. Gilbert was naïve and a novice when it comes to sex matters, or so she told O'Keeffe.

Gilbert was not too keen on the blessings of the church, though he supported the church financially. He believed that Igbo religion, *Odinani*, is superior to Eurocentric Christianity. He always wondered why every Christian wants to reach God through one man: Whatever happened to the concept of *Chi* guiding every soul's quest for a fulfilling life on earth? To him, the old men at the top echelon of church affairs were pseudo pagans fleeing from an authentic African creed that preaches a here-and-now judgment, not some damnation day in the skies. Imagine judging every Indian on that day, then all Chinese citizens that ever lived. Many local Catholics in those days did not read the Bible. Whatever the Catechist unraveled from what O'Keeffe said in English, with his heavy Irish accent, was all they knew.

For his mother's sake, Gilbert went ahead with the church wedding; for O'Keeffe's sake, Chināsa put on a brave face and pretended to be a devotee of Virgin Mary. The wedding was the biggest show since the colonial coronation of Chief Okéifè in 1917. In spite of all the bad airs and flamed eyes, many came calling—invited or not. Rainmakers threatened thunder and hailstone if Gilbert failed to see them. It was already early rainy season, and only hardheaded or foolish citizens ignored the threat of rainmakers to unleash rainstorm.

The rainmakers got their inflated fees. It did not rain.

Gilbert declared surplus, as they say in Nigeria. Many folks were still finding it hard to feed well, let alone buy beer. There were basins of freshly prepared foods, cartons of assorted beers, bottles of various wines and liquors, and jars of palm wine. The conniving church committee members left last. The younger committee members dragged their loots of unopened bottles of beer and fried goat meat along with their drunken spouses and tipsy children with bulging and shiny stomachs.

4

OBIAGÆLI WAS BORN AND BRED A VERY PRETTY princess fit for a king. Her father, *Nze* Chimé, was a prominent titled man and a merchant of immense wealth. He descended directly from the founder of the town, *Ichie* Chimé, though every indigene of the town is regarded as his offspring, hence the town's name, *Ụmụchimé*—the children of Chimé. As a young girl, Obiagæli lived up to her given Igbo name, *Ọ bịa ga-eli akụ,* which told the world that she came to enjoy wealth. At age 12, matchmakers claiming privileged and direct access to the family head had already lined up suitors.

In those days, secondary schools for girls were in faraway places. Nze Chimé refused to send his first daughter to live among strangers. He built a high school for her and opened it to everyone: boys, girls, and anyone considered eligible by the principal. Alas, Anglican missionary prudes prevailed on the colonial authority not to recognize a coed institution at high school level.

Gilbert Okonkwo Iké was the first principal of the school. He took on the colonial authorities and earned the name 'Mr. Ikékaiké,' in recognition of his 'super power.' He disregarded the non-recognition and argued that certificates are not a true measure of education. However, in the 1930s, British colonial administrators got their wish, especially when they had an ax to grind with the proprietor or principal of any school. The District Commissioner denied recognition. Nze Chimé was not an Anglophile; on the contrary, he was an anti-colonial Anglophobe extraordinaire.

The school closed.

Mr. Ikékaiké stayed back to teach Obiagæli at the large Chimé Estate. He cycled across from Eziuke, about four miles to the northeast. His wife had died. His only son Nnanna Iké was at a boarding school, but he spent his vacation at home. Nnanna became friendly with Obiagæli. He tutored her in sciences, at which his father was rusty.

Nze Chimé died quite unexpectedly in late 1939. He had numerous wives and many children, who were lost in the seas of sympathizers. Nnanna was there for Obiagæli. Two years later, Nnanna's father, Mr. Ikékaiké, died in a motor vehicle accident on the treacherous Udi Hill serpentine, also known as Milliken Hill. Nnanna was devastated. He needed all the help he could get. Obiagæli asked her brothers to help with the funeral expenses. The deceased had not only been her teacher and friend, he gave life to her best friend.

Obiagæli and Nnanna fell in love. He proposed marriage. He had his limitations. Like his father, he was a teacher—a poorly paid but respectful job. The Chimé clan chipped in to help with resources and with building of a new bungalow for the newly married. Chief Chima Chimé was supportive; he adored his junior sister. Sadly, for Nnanna—son of Gilbert Okonkwo Iké, alias Mr. Ikékaiké, the principal and private tutor—marrying a princess raised more than a few eyebrows; it consumed him.

Thirty years later, Obiagæli Iké, nee Chimé, was happy to see Chināsa, her successor, spitting here and there, her complexion yellowing as if she was coming down with juvenile jaundice. She had carried the cross of a luckless marriage for over a quarter of a century; it was time to drop it before it affected her son. Obiagæli was not that ill or old, but she knew she could soldier on no more. Whatever role God put her on earth to accomplish, she felt she had scored more than 50 percent at about age 50, a passing grade in her books. The rest was outside her locus of control.

Doctors said she will pull through and that her illness was more psychosomatic than physiological. To Gilbert, the phrase and many more medical explanations of test results were jargon-full analyses designed to make the big bills easier to swallow than petite pills.

On a Saturday, two months after the wedding, Gilbert got ready to attend a get-together in the village square. As time approached, his mother sent him to call her brother. They ate dinner and talked until Chināsa started tripping over to the other side of the living and back. Gilbert took her to their bed.

"Whatever happens, don't leave her," Gilbert's mother said as soon as he retook his seat beside her. "She is your wife, and she is also a girl-child of your mother, your *sister*."

"Don't talk like that, Mama. You know...."

"Just promise me, please."

"*O-o*, I promise."

"Good. The good Lord will bless you both. I may be far away, but...."

"Mama, you are going nowhere."

"Gilbert, listen to your mother."

Gilbert was surprised. His uncle, Chief Chima Chimé, with whom he shares the same first name—Chimaobim, had never spoken to him like a child. He sat back and listened.

"Thank you, brother Chima. My son, I shall always be with you. Nothing will happen to you. The sacrifices I have made must have touched someone up there. Do not *kill*... and I do not mean mere murder... murder is easy; spiritual killing is a sacrilegious stain. Never conspire against any person. Unguarded statements have driven many to early deaths. Whatever happens in life, there is a reason for it; often, it happens to teach you and others a lesson. Nobody is too old to learn. Life is not about what happened; it is about what you do with what happened. You hear what I am saying?"

Gilbert nodded.

She continued, "Your forefathers influenced communities from Amadike to Aniocha. They were great teachers. They never supported evil. They were not rich in material things, but they were warriors of light. The light entrusted to a child can never go out on him. Do not extinguish that light; on the contrary, make it shine brighter."

"Obiagæli, you don't mean he should become a teacher?"

"No, brother Chima," she said smilingly. "However, good teachers don't go about with chalks. You teach by example." The men nodded. "Now, my son, go and join your Eziuke people. I have something to discuss with my brother."

"Are you sure you will be okay, Mama?" She nodded. "Right, I'll see you very shortly then?"

"Sure, we'll see shortly, just don't disturb me when you come in. One more thing: if you drink even a glass of wine, sleep in another room. I don't want that girl to be hassled at all, or else you will not be seeing me."

She had never called Chināsa 'that girl,' not even in rare moments of anger. In contrast, the Igbo refer to a pregnant woman as 'an old woman,' probably because she exhibits some symptoms of old age. A characteristic of many Igbo dialects is that people make up their own style of speech and spice it with idioms. Older folks turn speeches into an art of communication that requires some studying to understand. Gilbert was not made of oratorical stuff, so he let it be.

When Chimé called very early the next morning, four hours after they had parted, Margaret Obiagæli Iké was gone. She passed on peacefully in her sleep. The wailing of women and the sobbing of sisters echoed across the land.

Chināsa was naturally devastated. She had made a mental note of the day she will give Obiagæli a child, which was why she took in as soon as Gilbert proposed. Alas, her mother-in-law and friend lived long enough to see the pregnancy through five difficult months.

What woman will see another through a messy abortion and still recommends her to an only son, her own son? Obiagæli trusted fate. To Chināsa, it was as if she had lost her own mother, a sister, and a friend, all rolled into an angel she affectionately called *'Mama de Mama'* — the woman who called her 'my daughter' and meant it. She was uncontrollable.

Gilbert was devastated, but the pain of death transformed quickly into concern for Chināsa's welfare. He remembered his mother's counsel vividly. Chināsa suddenly scooped up all the love he had for his mother. She was so much distressed that many did not expect her pregnancy to make it through the mourning period. Many women were sure she will lose the baby; debatable was whether she will survive it.

Chināsa's mother moved down south to be with her. Her stepfather and half-brother became regular visitors. Yet, the town held a lot of sadness yearning for fruits of forgetfulness. The rumors and gossips, she ignored; the pains, she endured; and now she had lost the one person who really cared for her. The rumor mills cranked up again.

Chief Chimé summed it up for her: "My dear daughter, the problem with Eziuke is that they have too many people with fired-up eyes. If you cry too much, they say you know what killed your beloved one, or you have no money for food and drinks. If you do not cry, they say you have always hated and despised the deceased, and that you were waiting for him or her to move on. We know none of these is true. You have mourned my sister, your sister, your mother, and your friend. It's time we moved on."

"Uncle, but what am I supposed to do!" she sobbed, her eyes swollen and her lips trembling.

"Woman, please follow your husband." It was not a direct answer to a question not asked; it was a polite command.

Chināsa packed.

"That woman recovered, eh?" one villager said to another as the draw of dust settled. The driver of Gilbert's Peugeot 404 was not speeding. They could see the popular passenger. "She has taken his mother to her early grave. The road is now clear to complete the assignment. Please mark my words: China, that female child of Abigail Ezenāgu, will see the end of Ikékaiké household. It is a shame!"

"Oh yes-o! Only Obiagæli the child of Chimé could have saved her son Gilbert Iké from the clutches she put on him."

"And now she is no more! That's what I am saying."

That Chināsa was an omen of misfortune defied rational explanations. The idle minds of Eziuke town could not easily reintegrate into an orderly postwar society. Their jeremiads had so far come to naught: Gilbert survived certain death—as they had forewarned, married, and lived to see her pregnant. Yet, they stuck to their gossip guns.

Obiagæli would have married Chināsa for Nnanna, her late husband, if Gilbert had not committed. Female same-sex marriage is an acceptable customary practice in Eziuke and environs. It is a community-sanctioned pact that has no hint of lesbianism when viewed with Western lenses. There is definitely no shade of sexual affair between the women. The necessity for such same-sex matrimony is for the younger woman to repopulate a dying dynasty. Chināsa would have been free to procreate with Gilbert. The products of the union would be his biological children but traditional half siblings. In that case, he would have been free to make a different choice of wife later in life and, as in many such cases, with Chināsa's blessing and sincere support.

All that was now academic; Gilbert loved her, and he was sticking with her. To her, not marrying into the Iké family was no longer an option; it was destined.

5

CHINĀSA HAD A PEACEFUL PREGNANCY. GILBERT shielded her as if a python's egg after the pregnancy threatened to abort, a situation her doctors contained. From the seventh month onwards, she coasted to delivery as if on a conveyor belt. The best medical hands in town were hired and nothing, humanly speaking, could go wrong.

Father O'Keeffe was around to offer prayers before she went into labor in early December 1971. He was not only her parish priest he was a confidante and a family friend. Routine confessions were no longer necessary because she confided in him as a friend. The sense of security from knowing that, theoretically, no one will ever hear whatever she said to him did wonders for Chināsa's confidence.

When the matron came out to make 'we have a baby girl' announcement, she expected the usual cold reception. She had seen it several times on the faces of first-time fathers whose wives delivered the *wrong* sex.

"Is this her first?" she asked, trying to cushion the effect of her impending announcement by blaming whom the society said was at fault—the mother.

Gilbert nodded and said, "Yes?"

"You won't have to worry about the tax man yet."

"Brilliant! Thank you, Almighty God!" he shouted with excitement. He then held his hands together and quietly prayed to *Chineke*, the Creator.

"This one must be different," a nurse quipped.

"Don't mind him," the matron mused. "Bridewealth does not amount to much these days."

"Matron, that's my Mom in there; may I see her?"

She shrugged and waved him on with a suspiciously dismissive demeanor, wondering what sort of a modern man he was. Gilbert wanted no mix-ups. He knew that such an incident was remote, but it could happen. He had arranged for a secluded special delivery at home, but the consultant counseled against it.

"It is her first, and she has gone through some stress. Anything can go wrong," the consultant had said.

Nothing went wrong. Gilbert requested and got an early release. Two nurses were already waiting at home, and he retained his doctor to check on mother and child every day. It was not necessary, but he was paying. He was an only child, the one product of an only pregnancy. His mother had given him her all. Everything she ever did from the night she conceived him, she did for him. Everything he had done since she departed was in readiness for this day.

Gilbert did not say, 'Oh, Mama, I wish you were here'; it was as if he was actually talking to his mother. It is customary to pay such compliments, an act of reverence to a beloved, blessed dear departed. To Gilbert, it was actually his mother starting life again after undergoing a biological makeover. Igbo traditional creed concurs; it accepts that the difference between life and death is nine months.

Gilbert planned the naming ceremony like a festival. He spared no cost. His business was booming. Only recent family matters kept him from expanding to other cities. He was targeting Lagos before making a move for overseas market. Money was no problem.

Crates of bottled drinks, kegs of palm wine, and huge pots of assorted fresh foods started arriving with city cocks crowing at dawn. Gilbert contracted out all cooking duties to avoid hassles, the sort of hassles encountered at occasions held in Eziuke. He was not disappointed.

The reverend sisters at Mother of Christ Convent paid attention to every grain of rice, practically designed every piece of meat, and made the *egusi* and okra soups look like Archangel Michael and his angels were coming to supper.

Family, friends, and friendly folks came bearing befitting gifts. Those who knew Gilbert from Eziuke understood why he was over the hilltop with excitement.

When the naming ceremony commenced, he called her Nnénnaya ('mother of her father'). As is tradition, Grandma Abigail called her Nénné ('good mother'). They obliged her, but Chimé pointed out that Ezinné [same as Nénné, which may be confused with Nnénné—'mother of (her) mother'] was more their dialect of Igbo language. Guests looking for an excuse to show how little the war affected their deep pockets and openhandedness supported. Other equally loaded guests objected to the semantics.

On such occasions, customary considerations cease and age takes a backseat. The magic of money speaks loudly. Money literally rained and reigned. Madaki was there with his business associates to support his wife and her choice of name for their granddaughter. Fanny was the chief of protocol, and nothing went wrong from her end.

By the end of the day, it was Ezinné Nnénna. Gilbert bought both names: His mother was the best. His wife was a paragon of peace. His mother-in-law was a pillar of support. All round, it was a colossal celebration of motherhood and womanhood.

"I thank you all for gracing this occasion," Gilbert began in his closing remarks. "I won't bore you with my feelings...."

"Speak!" a gatecrasher urged with drunken rudeness.

"This is not an everyday event. It is a once-in-a-life-time thing." Gilbert talked about the bundle of joy in his strong arms for thirty good minutes. It was his party, and it was happening in his house. Nobody complained.

"This is the most wonderful thing to have happened to me ever: my mother's return. I thank you for being a part of this occasion. Finally...." Murmurs of relief echoed; folks wanted to continue the merrymaking. "Finally, ladies and gentlemen, the old and the young, I present to you all, to all the dear deities, and to our estimable elders gone before us, my one and only Ezinné Nnénna: my daughter, my mother."

"Ezinné Nnénna!" everyone hailed.

Applause and good wishes from everyone ensued. Guests who knew Gilbert very well understood what he meant. To the majority, he was just happy that he had a female child, which meant that an out-of-this-world party awaited the arrival of a male.

"May it please *Chiukwu*, God Almighty, who gave her to us, that she grows up with a special *Chi* behind and before her, an invisible but benevolent guardian angel to guard and guide her through the wilderness of life...."

"*Isée!*" everybody agreed.

"And may the good Lord grant her everything good... one God forever and ever...."

"Amen!"

It was a wonderful start for the Christmas season, a naming ceremony like no other before it. It signaled the beginning of a new era, the era of unabashed materialism and prosperity—a firm foot on the road to the famous but failed "3R": reconciliation, rehabilitation, and reconstruction. To the elders, it was like the first harvest from the ashes of the sad civil crises—a new beginning, as if the fateful fratricidal fracas that wrecked lives and properties was an awful tree of thorns that bore some fine fruits.

Alas, the mad rush to spend the proceeds of oil boom ensued and dawned the decadence and doom of generations yet unborn. Things never remained the same again.

6

EZENĀGU FAMILY WAS OF THE ANGLICAN FAITH. Chināsa and her mother returned to the faith while in London. She had no hang-ups about religions, but her stepfather's faith is not a middling Middle Eastern religion; it is a way of life that was alien to hers. Lately, Chināsa was no longer keen on organized religions and their rituals.

Gilbert was not too keen on foreign religions. His family was Catholic, but his mother did not feel that the church dealt her a fair hand when she needed it. He resented the church for that, but no 1970s ex-Biafran person wanted to be tagged a 'pagan.' It was as if the reason why God made the East to lose the war was its laidback acceptance of Jesus Christ. Everyone now identified with his church. It was like a social club, a place to be, especially on the Sunday of every month that is *Eke* day on Igbo customary calendar.

Gilbert still supported the Catholic Church parishes in Enugu and in Eziuke. A delegation usually delivered special invitations for big events, such as the annual Thanksgiving & Bazaar. Members of every delegation were guaranteed booze and mouthwatering dishes. Parish priests personally chased pledges with unannounced visits and telephone calls.

After the traditional naming ceremony, Chināsa gradually drifted to Anglican friends. At first, it was for thanksgiving services. When Gilbert raised no objection, she stopped coming up with excuses. Nonetheless, she still paid or, rather, he paid their Catholic AMC and other dues at both their home church and city parishes. Nobody said what 'AMC' was, but Gilbert figured it was their annual membership contribution, a fee for keeping the poor spiritually satisfied.

A couple of weeks before the baptismal ceremony, Chināsa began to search for a unique name for their daughter. Friends suggested such simple names as Susanna or Mercy, compound names—Rosemary, MaryAnn, or Maria Goretti, names of saints—Perpetua and Agatha, biblical names–Naomi, Rebecca, and Ruth, names of queens—Elizabeth and Catherine, and princesses—Anne and Stephanie. Chināsa was not impressed.

"What sort of name do you want?" Fanny asked.

"When I hear or see it, I'll know. I am looking for a name that rings a loud bell: exotic, sexy, and chique."

Four days before the sacrament at the local St Anthony's, she drove herself to the Anglican All Saints. The pastor was very understanding and happy to help, after receiving a trunkload of fruits and vegetables, a big red cockerel, and seven huge Abakaliki yams. He had books and dictionaries of names. If he had none, he would have typed out one.

"I thank you very much," he told Chināsa before leaving her alone, "soldering for Christ will not succeed on a flat diet. The Catholic priests have driven the point home for all men of the cloth. They enjoy as if there is no tomorrow, as if heaven is on earth."

Chināsa was not interested in denominational divide or the implicit disparity in fringe benefits. She wanted a name for her daughter. She sat down in the pastor's large lounge with a mountain of literature for two hours. She was not interested in whomever the names belonged or how they came to be; she just wanted a special name.

"Seek and you shall find it," she kept muttering to herself. She finally found *it* under the letter 'F.'

Gilbert came back early for the baptismal ceremony on a Friday, but their appointment was cancelled.

"Why?" he asked, showing no great disappointment.

"They said the name I chose is not a saint's name."

"Why didn't you phone your boyfriend?"

"Who is my 'boyfriend'?" Chināsa snapped.

"The one you told when you conceived the child."

"Father O'Keeffe? Don't you start," Chināsa giggled. "Anyway, I did. Surprised?" He shook his head. "The parish secretary said he is not back. He traveled to Dublin to see his superiors and later see his folks in Ireland."

"Okay, what did the city parish priest say we should do to wash away the original sin from the chick?"

"He said I must choose another name. He gave me names of old mamas in the village. My child cannot answer to Agatha or Gertrude. Imagine the nonsense!"

"Come on, Chināsa, you worry too much. It does not matter what name they like; no one calls her anything in this house but Nnénna, or Ezinné—if your mother comes around. So, my dear, relax." Gilbert wanted to suggest his mother's Christian name, but that would push Chināsa into a corner. She would have agreed.

"I am sorry, but that priest has no right to choose a name for my baby. Children are special; they cannot be lumbered with names that do not mean much, do not sound right and, for all we know, tell stories that do not relate to us. The sacrament of baptism should allow parents a wider degree of choice in naming their children."

"I don't worry about sacraments; commandments, I like... except the sixth—which I feel like fouling again." Gilbert put his arms round her waist.

"Stop it, Giles. We are still talking about cleansing the *fouling* from earlier last year."

They laughed until the baby woke up and called for their attention the only way she knew.

They both rushed into her room to find the babysitter fast asleep beside her. They took the baby upstairs and left the little housemaid to sleep.

They were having dinner in their kitchenette, after taking care of dirty diapers. Chināsa kept complaining: "The goat I was going to give them on Sunday will now be slaughtered and cooked here. A fresh, peppered *isiewu* delicacy won't go down the wrong way, you know."

Gilbert chuckled loudly at the thought of the goat-head delicacy that she hated. "Their loss is my gain."

She was still in a fighting mood. "No, I know what to do. It will go to God in another church. I wanted to wait for Charlie... Father O'Keeffe to come back, but Fanny is leaving for the United States of America next week."

He looked surprised. "What has she got to do...."

"She is the godmother, remember?"

He did not know; it did not matter: Fanny was her best friend. Chināsa did not forget how she came to her help when she needed help most. Gilbert recognized Fanny's friendship and support. He had helped her countless times without telling his wife. He gave her his bank statements with which she processed her visa to America and for the university admission formalities. He did not tell Chināsa because it was no big deal.

Gilbert decided to pay for her flight ticket, and he told Chināsa. She was thrilled: "Giles, you don't know how this makes me feel."

He knew.

As a busy business executive, Gilbert traveled a lot, but he provided for his family. Chināsa did not have to lift a finger. She had babysitters and houseboys who ran errands. Her mother Abigail spent time in and around Enugu. Chināsa had everything she wanted, but she envied Fanny, a fiercely independent and assertive woman who apparently knew exactly what she wanted from life and how to get it.

7

CHINELO CIRCUMVENTED THE CATHOLIC CHURCH, chose, and called her daughter 'Finlay.' No one had heard of the name, but Chināsa was adamant. It is an English name; a princess or a queen, no one in town knew.

Gilbert was not perturbed: "It is the wife's scene," he told his friend Yerima. "The child will forever be Nnénna, the second coming of my mother made perfect."

The special, colorful ceremony of baptism tempted Gilbert to consider switching allegiance to the Anglican Communion. He could not; his mother would turn in her grave. The Catholic Church might not have been fair to her, but she believed in what it says about the Madonna and her child in *Hail Mary*. Gilbert's mother hailed Mary because she was almost like the Virgin, but the angel that visited her in mid-1940s made contact, the only sexual contact she ever had with a man. Virgin Mary fared better; she bore children for the Nazarene carpenter called Joseph.

Chināsa's action angered Chief Chimé and his wife. They accused her of sowing the seed of disunity in the family. Gilbert saw no need for the fuss, but he and Chināsa listened. The Chimés were indeed their pillars of support in moments of misery and sundry needs. She apologized and promised that as long as she lived, she will never take the child into an Anglican church.

As soon as the dust raised by Chināsa began to settle, another problem emerged. The state government arrested and accused Gilbert of embezzling funds while he worked with the ministry of agriculture before the war.

It was down to Chimé, again.

Chief Chimé was a successful business executive with a strong base in the city. He hired a young lawyer, Anthony Ikpeama, to lock horns with the equally young prosecutor. Tony Ikpeama exposed the case for what it was—a vendetta. In the process, he paved his way to fame and fortune.

Finlay Ezinné Nnénna Iké grew up in comfort. No other issue came along a long time after her; not for lack of trying, but nature has a weird way of playing tricks. Gilbert was not worried, but Chināsa was a bag of worries. He prospered and expanded across the waters. Bone-lazy rumormongers had explanations and more predictions of doom. Gilbert was not interested in what people said. The happiness that Nnénna brought to his life was immeasurable.

Chināsa was under family and social pressures to produce a male. The pressure from society was mostly subtle, but it was there. Therefore, wherever supposed miracles happened, Chināsa was there: native doctors, fertility clinics, spiritual churches, and prayer houses. If mosques were to promise some relief, she would have gone there, but Muslims leave everything to Allah. Her mother warned her sternly that no one could change what God has destined. Her stepfather counseled that she had no say in the matter. Chināsa ignored them. She became a hostage in the house of hope.

Gilbert supported his wife, on the understanding that he will not accompany her to 'miracle houses' nor swallow any concoction, modern or native. He made it clear that she must not put portions of medication in their food. She respected his wishes. The consequences of a family feud were too much to contemplate.

The worries of Chināsa did not remove from her love for FEN, as she called Nnénna; she was all they had. Why she raised all the dust with 'Finlay,' no one asked her. Faustina, Franca, Felicia, or Fatima could have given her the letter 'F.' To Gilbert, Nnénna was all he had and all he wanted.

Nnénna had everything and everybody spoiled her, from her father's business associates to his friends and down the line to favor-seekers, freeloaders, sycophants, bootlickers, and hangers-on. Beautiful and intelligent, she could do no wrong in her father's eyes. She grew up with a much more beautiful complexion than her mother's quarter-to-albino skin texture. She inherited her father's height and strong bones. Plaiting her hair took a full day. Chināsa gave up the duty very early in Nnénna's life. The brightness of her teeth competed with the flash of lightening.

She was a special child, always poised and emotionally balanced. With her father, there were no pretences and no airs. Gilbert wanted her to grow up like every other child—normal. He did not want her to grow up in social isolation, as most uptown parents wanted of their children.

Chināsa was always going and coming from child search she spent little time with Nnénna, who got most of her preschool education from various househelps. Elegant and bright, she went to a posh private nursery school in town. After kindergarten, Gilbert registered her in a public primary school. Chināsa agreed, or she was too busy to care anyway.

One evening, Chināsa sat exhausted in front of television eating fruits. Gilbert played hide and seek with Nnénna. Even when Nnénna hid behind her, Chināsa ignored them. After the third find, he stopped and wanted to know if Nnénna learnt anything at school that day. The girl thought about it and said she heard a new song. He wanted to hear it. She hesitated, and then she started to sing:

> *Daddy, do you want to know my name,*
> *Mommy, do you want to know my name,*
> *My name is ... Chi-Chi Chikito*
> > *Lo - Lo Lovito*
> *If you ask my Papa and my Mama,*
> *All the young boys call me 'Apaama'!*

Gilbert was laughing as Nnénna explained that she thought the song—popular with urban, all-girl street dancers called 'Erico Angels'—was silly. Chināsa was boiling over and fuming as Nnénna sang. Her anger swelling, she waited for Gilbert to stop laughing before confronting the poor girl.

"Is that what they taught you at school today?" Chināsa yelled in Igbo. Nnénna had never seen her mother so angry; she was surprised and looked it. "Answer me now: Is that what you go out to learn?"

Gilbert sat up: "Chill it, Chichi. It is just a poem."

"Poem… you call that a poem? Poem is 'Twinkle, twinkle, little star, /How I wonder what you are. /Up above the world so high, /Like a diamond in the sky.' Do you get it?"

"Go on, Chichi, go on and educate us!"

"Poem is 'The vulture eats between his meals, /And that's the reason why /He very, very rarely feels /As well as you and I. /His eye is dull, his head is bald, /His neck is growing thinner. /Oh! what a lesson for us all /To only eat at dinner."

"Bravo! Okay?"

"That's kid's poetry, not the nonsense some half-baked teacher dreams up and feeds to unsuspecting children."

"Chichi, it's children playground song. The teachers can't do anything about that. Have you forgotten your own Erico days? Kids from downtown still…."

"Giles, I don't care what they do downtown. My child is not going back to that state farm for future social rejects. Now 'Miss Angelica Erico,'" Chināsa commanded coldly, "Go to your room and don't let me hear that song from your mouth ever again. Do you hear me?"

Nnénna looked at her father. He nodded. She ran up to her room. Gilbert went after her and stayed with her until she was ready for bed. He came back thereafter and told Chināsa in a very simple language that she would leave his house if she ever talked to Nnénna like that.

"Ever!" he bellowed.

Chināsa protested that she wanted Nnénna to have the best education and threatened to take her to another school. He was done. She could do whatever else she liked.

Gilbert was not the book type, but he took time to check the classic lyrics of Jane Taylor (1783-1824) and Hilaire Belloc (1870-1953) that his wife had referenced and more. Admitted that they are popular classics from yesteryears, it should not stop the development of popular classics of tomorrow today. He recalled numerous Erico songs that could pass for poems, but no one thought of compiling and publishing them. He also remembered many songs his mother and her mates sang; those too could pass for poems.

He chuckled as he recalled a certain after-meeting chant popular with women groups, especially after glasses of sweet palm wine. The trendy song appeals to folks—brethren and kinfolk—to do what pleases the singer's heart, not use teasers or indirect idioms to address her concerns because they are unacceptable to human decency:

> *Umunne m na umunna m-o*
> *Gee nu nti:*
> *Umunne m na umunna m-o*
> *Gee nu nti:*
> *Onye mara ihe na-adi m mma n'obi*
> *Ya mee ya*
> *Ma onye ejine njakiri na-agwa m okwu*
> *Ahu m achoghi ya!*

Nnénna did not lack for attention; she got surplus supply from her father. Her introduction to family friendship came with Barrister and Mrs. Ikpeama's family. Zina, their only daughter, grew up with everything her mates saw in dreams. The world of her parents revolved around her. She was the sparkle in their eyes, the precious stone in their matrimonial tiara. Her friends looked forward to her birthday bash and other weekend parties as they did Christmas.

Nnénna's friendship with Zina was more an association of circumstance and convenience than true friendship. Of note, their common situation did not bother both fathers, who had become friends after the trial that nearly derailed Gilbert's entire entrepreneurial enterprise. Their wives did all the running around looking for male children in all the wrong places. Neglected and denied their mothers' full love, both girls found solace elsewhere: Zina in her books and Nnénna in her father's great admiration and expectation.

The girls got along okay, but there was nothing special about their friendship. The only child factor probably drew them closer more than any other factor of common interest or even the fact that Gilbert was Tony's client and friend.

London-born Zina was two years older and two classes ahead of Nnénna, and this helped Nnénna to grow up faster. On the other side, Nnénna could not quite figure out Zina, whose attitude highlighted high-order hypocrisy. Zina talked as if she had calculated every simple sentence, as if there was much more left unsaid than said. A voracious reader, Zina had a sound knowledge base that is far beyond her years. It made communicating with her peers sometimes difficult.

8

Nnénna went to Queen's High School, a meeting point of social snobs reared to believe in a concept of class that is alien to the indigenous Igbo people of Enugu. Though many of its students were from levelheaded and conservative Christian homes, the few bad apples set the social scene agog with 'setting standards,' making those whose parents scratched and borrowed to put there to curse the day they chose Queen's High.

The top all-girl high school had girls whose parents were movers and shakers of society, the crèmes de la crème, but Nnénna made them look more like creams of the crap. She had no special friends, but she tried her best to be good to everyone. The culture at Queen's did not accept such rugged republicanism: either you were the best of the rest, in which case others toiled to catch up, or you were 'below standard' and trying to catch up with others.

Nnénna did not succumb to the status quo. Some girls talked big, claiming control of colored clouds, but they were pillagers of pencils and pens. Those were out of her galaxy: too ordinary and near fake. Many whose parents were rich could not resist the urge to flaunt it. They too were out of her loop: too shallow and too spoilt.

Those who craved attention, she ignored. She interacted more with those who hailed from poor background and were neither proud nor ashamed of it. She did not intend to invite anyone home, and she was not keen on visiting any of the girls. Essentially, she progressed through high school without exploiting her background.

Nnénna remained a mystery for three years. She ignored both sides of the silly aisle of set standards, but no one ignored her. Love her or loathe her, she had an innate quality nobody overlooked: She had class, a natural class that neither breeding nor money can bequeath on sewer turtles. Her social sophistication was so transparent yet difficult to figure out in teenage Nnénna.

One day in the school's staff room, a staffer said that someone she had met reminded her of the 'spoilt rottenness of Finlay Iké.' They called Nnénna 'Finlay' in school, courtesy of her mother who made it her first name in kindergarten.

"Wait a minute," a senior male tutor gasped in protest. "The girl is many things, but she is neither spoilt nor rotten."

Nnénna's housemistress and French tutor supported the male tutor's assertion. The others agreed. They gave their reasons, but not one of them knew what stood her apart from other students. Everyone agreed that she was not arrogant; she just did not think much of certain things.

"The thing about Finlay Nnénna Iké is probably why a French phraseologist formulated the phrase, *'je ne sais quoi.'* There is definitely an indescribable special something about her." The mademoiselle should know; she had just come back from a three-month refresher course in Abidjan, the capital of Côte d'Ivoire. Case closed.

The senior girls resented Nnénna's attitude, deeming it contemptuous. They knew little about her background, apart from the fact that 'her dad is on.' Everything they knew about her came from unreliable gossip mills. There were no city tabloids to confirm such news items. Nnénna made sure her parents did not come around to parade cars and clothes at Queen's. Her mother, whose menstruation period had not missed a second in fourteen years, was still busy searching for a boy. Her father went deeper into international wheeling and dealing; he now spent more time traveling.

Only Zina Ikpeama was close. She knew Nnénna down to her bedroom in the village, but she was her senior in school. At Queen's, it was not normal for students in different grades to socialize as equals. For some reason, Zina wanted her to respect the rule. Nnénna respected the unvoiced wish.

Nnénna was good at giving everyone a chance to prove herself. She had given Zina so many chances and seen the aura of a double-crosser about her, the aura of a captain who will bail out with the lone lifeboat and take the only lifejacket along with it, and the aura of someone worthy of distrust. Zina always looked like she was withholding something, as if everything must be about her and only about her. Nnénna made a special effort to maintain a relationship with Zina throughout her days at Queen's. She avoided Zina when she was in the company of her classmates, and Zina seemed to appreciate the gesture.

Nnénna was in boarding school, but she came home every visiting day and on most weekends. Gilbert was away quite a lot, but he spent far more quality time with Nnénna than an above-average father spent with his son. All business deals took a backseat on her visiting days. 'Visiting days' meant that Nnénna visited home, not her parents visiting her. The principal granted the concession because Nnénna was the best-behaved student, and she (the principal) had a special relationship with her father.

There was no pressure on Nnénna to behave well or to do well in school. She did better than expected on both counts. Her mother's contribution so far was to make sure everybody, except herself, called her 'Finlay.' To Gilbert, she remained his mother reliving her life with all the freedom and comfort his money could provide. He wanted his daughter to get some education, not to become an encyclopedia, so they rarely discussed academia. They were that into themselves.

Nnénna was always ahead of her class. She came third in Oral English in the last term of fourth year. The principal's daughter and another girl, both of expatriate or been-to parentage, set the standard. The teacher, who boasted of an expatriate lecturer at the University of Ibadan in the 1960s, seemed to prefer any pronunciation with foreign tinge to it than the actual pronunciation of words. Colleagues called it 'cowed colonial carriage.'

Nnénna arrived back in school for the final year. Parents milled around with their flashy cars and their bespectacled ugly daughters, some with teeth held together with wires. The girls wore dazzling clothes and paraded gadgets and toys. She walked out of the dilapidated 404 and made it look like a Rolls Royce. She smiled as she disembarked, the driver holding the door. He helped her with her box, but Nnénna took over after a short distance, telling the driver to go and earn some money for his family. It used to be his father's car before she was born, his first car, but it had since converted to a city cab to help the poor distant relation.

The first term, Nnénna stretched her lead in every subject—spoken or written. The new English teacher was a different dry die. A graduate of English from USA, she was not interested in the crude cockney accent of the London-born girl who had beaten everyone, or in the Germanic inflections of the principal daughter's accent. The new teacher wanted words pronounced correctly. Accents did not count in her records. 'War-ah' or 'war-rah' no longer passed for 'water.' The 't' in 'what' became compulsory. The 'g' in every gerund got a strange pronunciation that nobody actually mastered. In the end, it was preferred to say 'nothingg,' not 'nothin'.'

Nnénna had a good command of pronunciations: Long before many people saw colored television, she owned a videocassette player/recorder. Gilbert lived for her. Every effort he put into the trials of life was for his only child.

9

CHINĀSA FOUND OUT THE HARD WAY THAT SHE and her daughter had grown apart. She drove into Queen's one evening with the latest Nippon wonder machine and dressed like a hot Hollywood homemaker. The principal escorted her to the field, where some students were playing netball while others watched. The cheers ceased. The jeers jammed. The players stood still. Nnénna saw her mother and wanted to hide.

"Miss Finlay Iké," the German-born principal called out rather loudly.

The physical education teacher waved Nnénna out of the field, but she stood watching with her players in awe. No one spoke as Nnénna walked up to the two women and looked at her mother, disbelief written all over her face. She sighed slightly rudely and walked past to get as far away from the principal as was possible.

Chināsa followed her. "Darling FEN, what is it?" she asked sweetly as she struggled to catch up with her daughter, her high-heeled shoes taking the strain.

Nnénna stopped suddenly and faced her mother: "Mom, what on earth are you doing here?"

"Darling FEN, you know your father has opened an office in Hong Kong...."

"So?"

"I personally picked him up from Emene Airport... first flight from Lagos. I felt you will want to see some photos and the beautiful things he bought for you."

"Mom, you were not supposed to visit me. We agreed, didn't we? No, you wait a minute! Please, please just go."

"What?"

"Mom!"

"Okay, okay...." Chināsa could not believe it, but she knew Gilbert would be offended if he heard she visited and distressed her. "When will you come home?"

"This weekend... didn't Daddy tell you that much?"

It dawned on Chināsa that she had let her daughter to grow into a woman without really knowing her. In her blind drive to get her a brother, or rather a son for her husband, she had all but ignored her. The sort of bond that existed between Nnénna and her husband was too strong, but she had never been so bothered until this day.

Chināsa stood speechless as Nnénna walked back to her team, her eyes moist. She did not realize the principal had rejoined her.

"Is everything okay, Ma'am?" the principal asked. Still in her early forties, Mrs. Eva Olisa, born Bürgler, looked like something out of the history book of colonial West Africa. It was very hard to imagine that the woman started life in Bavaria, Germany. She was so at home in Enugu the city looked younger. An excellent administrator, she believed in learning something new every day.

"No... no, it's all right. Thanks very much for letting me see her." Chināsa turned, removed her shades, and dried the wet polychromatic lenses. She got into the car and drove off as if she had just won the Le Mans Rally.

"Finlay, is she your senior sister?" a classmate asked.

"It's none of your bloody business," Nnénna blurted.

"Okay, everybody back to your original positions," the physical education teacher ordered.

Students found out the following day that the flashy visitor was Nnénna's mother, thanks to the principal's daughter, Carla Olisa.

Nnénna came home on Friday evening. Her mother was waiting to give her an earful. Nnénna was ready for her. Gilbert was still in his city office, so the coast was clear for a battle of the Amazons: mother and daughter.

"Young lady," Chināsa began, unable to wait any longer for Nnénna to finish her after-dinner mixed-fruit salad, her favorite dessert. "I don't know what got into you last Wednesday, but let it be the first and last time you talk to me that way." Nnénna said nothing. "I hope you don't think I am talking to myself."

"No, ma'am, you are not talking to yourself."

"Now, clean that table before your Daddy comes in."

"Yes ma'am." Nnénna smiled. They had enough helps to do the cleaning, cooking, and waiting on the madam, yet Nnénna did not allow them to do things she could do for herself. She was washing plates for as far back as she could remember, long before they got a dishwasher. She grew up with babysitters, slept with them, and ate with them. They were her senior sisters. Telling her to clean the table was new and needless.

"FEN, you are developing some very bad attitudes. You are not going to get far in life with that kind of behavior. I am your mother! Don't you ever forget that."

"Yes, Mother."

"And stop speaking to me in that *murder* tone!"

"Okay, that's it," she said and got up. "You want to fight, wait for your husband. I'll be in my room if you need me." Calmly and coolly, she walked up the stairs.

"Finlay, come back here. Now!" Chināsa yelled as soon as she got her composure back. This was the only time she used the name for which she caused so much trouble, the sexy and exotic name that was so special she risked a rift just found some use in the house.

"My name is not 'Finlay'," Nnénna protested.

"I say, come back here before I make you do it!"

Nnénna stopped. She wanted to scream back at her; instead, she said calmly, "You want to talk, wait until Daddy gets home." She walked the few feet to her door, entered, and locked the door.

Chināsa came up the stairs. Nnénna's cassette player was blasting pop music. The volume was high. She shouted and pounded on the door until she was red. She wanted Nnénna to shout back and do something, anything but ignore her. She threatened to give her a good beating whenever she got her hands on "those two braless tangerines that give you the idea that we are women and equal before my husband."

"We are not; I am more equal," Nnénna shouted back. "And who needs bras, by the way?"

"What?!"

"You heard."

"That's it: I am smashing this door! I will break…."

"Chichi, what is it?" Gilbert had come in.

"Giles, you should come and talk to this mini monster before she becomes a real devil."

"Stop talking about Nnénna like that, woman!" he bellowed and then pleaded, "Please let her be."

Nnénna giggled loudly from inside her room.

"I see! You now enable her to insult me. Is it because I have not given you a son? What have I not done to give you a son? What else does she want? My life?"

"Oh, just shut up, Chichi, and come down here."

Gilbert had never spoken to his wife like that and definitely not to the hearing of their daughter. Chināsa walked down the corridor to the master bedroom and locked herself inside. She sulked. She knew not what else to do. If it were a niece, a cousin, or a half-sister, she would understand her feelings. "For goodness sake," she mumbled to reassure herself, "she is our daughter."

Gilbert took off his coat, washed his hands, and fixed himself a drink. He walked up the stairs and stopped at Nnénna's door. He listened to Michael Jackson's *Startin' Somethin'* and smiled. He tapped gently on the door.

"Mommy love, it's Daddy."

She opened the door and fell on him. "Hello Daddy, I'm sorry...."

"It's all right, Mommy. Please lower that nice noise." She turned it off. "Good. How are you, my dear?"

"You know...."

"Yes, I know about your Mom coming to the school and all that. Mrs. Olisa called my office soon after."

"She didn't tell you?"

"No, your Mom did not; she didn't mean any harm though. It won't happen again, believe me."

"Daddy, I really didn't say anything to hurt her."

"It doesn't matter. I'll sort it out with her."

They talked about the Hong Kong office and the things he bought for her: dresses, a camera, videotapes, games, and all sorts of things with her name embossed on them. She sat with her head on his chest for the one hour they talked and laughed and talked.

"Sir, the food is ready," the new maid announced.

"Is Madam there?"

"No sir." The latest addition to the army of housemaids rarely said more than required, a result of madam's strict order.

"Daddy, go and eat. I'll talk to China, child of Abigail Ezenāgu, woman to woman."

"Who... what?" Realizing that she just mentioned his wife by first and maiden names, as villagers preferred, he smiled. "Hey, don't use that name to her hearing."

"Daddy, what are you talking about? This is a woman who called her daughter 'Finlay'." They laughed. "Go on and enjoy your dinner. I'll sort her out."

Gilbert laughed so loudly Nnénna wondered why he was having so much fun at the expense of his wife, her mother. Definitely, it was not what she had said. She took the glass to the kitchenette and walked back to see him belly laughing as he tried to gain entrance into his matrimonial chamber.

"Come on, Chichi love, open up."

Nnénna motioned him to allow her. He obliged and walked down to the ground-floor dinning room. She waited for a minute or so before knocking on the door very gently. "Mom, please, it's me."

"What do you want? Go away."

She went to her room and fetched her portable cassette player. She tiptoed to the lounge and got a tape from their music library. Coming up the stairs, she tried the cassette player for power. The battery was flat. There was a socket in the corridor. She plugged in an extension cord and took it down the hallway to the door of the master bedroom.

Placing the gadget in front of the master bedroom's door, she depressed <PLAY> button. Prince Nico Mbarga and his 1976 Rocafil Jazz Band took over:

> *Sweet Mother, I no go forget you*
> *For this suffer wey you suffer for me -o,*
> ....
> *If I no sleep, my mother no go sleep,*
> *If I no chop, my mother no go chop,*
> *she no dey tire oh.*
> *Sweet Mother, oh-o, Sweet Mother oh-o.*

10

"MOM, WE MUST TALK, PLEASE," NNÉNNA SAID after four minutes of the Nigerian mothers' special. She turned down the volume and listened. "Please, Mommy...." The door opened as if 'mommy,' which she had never used since primary school, was the secret code.

"What do you want to talk about?"

"I'm sorry about what happened both at school and here this evening." She followed her into the large bedroom in which she had not been for a long, long time. "Mom, that was not me; you should have known that."

"So you now have Multiple Personality Syndrome?"

"What did you expect when you called me 'Finlay'?" She saw the bitterness in her eyes and smiled. "Joke, Mom."

"FEN, your behavior was inexcusable." Her voice was now conciliatory. "Are you ashamed of us?"

"How can I be ashamed of you? No one in that school has a mother like you. They thought you were my senior sister. I just don't like showing off, that's all. I don't want to look like a fickle-minded baby."

"Okay, that's your opinion; I respect that, but that does not excuse your attitude these days."

"What attitude, Mom?" She sat down. "Listen to me: You don't know what attitude I had and what attitude I now have. Surprised?" Nnénna sounded like she was talking to a mate.

Chināsa was surprised. "What do you mean?"

"Did you ever ask me how I coped with my first period?"

"You told Daddy, didn't you?"

"I did, indeed."

"Good."

"Mom, listen to yourself: 'You told Daddy'! Did you tell your father during your own time? You noticed bloodstains, you were bleeding, and you ran to your father. And Grandma never asked you how you coped?"

There was no father to tell, but Nnénna did not know that. As far as she knew, Alhaji Madaki was Grandma's husband, though she knew he was not her mother's biological father.

Chināsa said nothing.

"You see what I mean? You were going and coming from spiritual churches you missed my leaving for Queen's. I doubt you know that I skipped class six. Believe me, Mom, I understand what you are going through."

"FEN, please don't try to understand what I am going through because you won't succeed."

"At least, I understand that this issue of not having a son creates problems between you and Daddy. There is always a solution, you know."

"Please, it's enough. One day, you will understand. I am no longer angry. Go and join your Daddy."

"You see, it's always 'Go and join your Daddy'!" she mimicked light-heartedly. "Talk to me, Mom, no matter how stupid I sound. You said back there that I don't wear bras. Have you ever told me what they are? No, Daddy also had to buy my first bras; of course, he bought your size."

Chināsa tried to stifle a laugh. Her bosom to Nnénna's compared like melon to mango. Nnénna followed her eyes and looked at the lumps on her chest. "I'm sorry," Chināsa offered. She smiled and then let the laughter loose.

Nnénna laughed too. "You see what I mean? We are just like neighbors; at best, we look like squabbling sister-wives. What mother and daughter sit down to compare breasts? Not even our ancestors thought of that. I will explain: I have heard the expression, 'I'm not going to stand and measure manhood with you,' but not breasts."

"Watch you mouth, young lady," Chināsa cautioned for her use of the raw Igbo term for 'penis.' It hit her that Nnénna was right. She listened as if they were friends. Surprisingly, Nnénna knew more about life than Chināsa believed possible at her age. She felt relieved that somebody, especially her own daughter, understood what she was going through. Her husband understood too, but he readily dismissed her worries. Nnénna understood and counseled her.

"Did you say there is a solution?"

"Solutions, Mom. One, if you are sure there is nothing wrong with you, then it's Daddy. Travel with him next month and insist you see a doctor abroad. Tests may reveal that he has a low sperm count."

"What?"

"Or the sperms are healthy but have weak propulsion to get to the eggs in the fallopian tube."

"Stop!"

"Mom, we study these things in school, and there are living-color videotapes. Did you watch *From Cradle to Coffin*?" Chināsa shook her head. "You must, Mom; it is educative. There is a copy in Dad's studio. It tells the whole story with dramatic scenes from inside the womb."

Chināsa flinched and said, "You watched it?"

Nnénna ignored the question and said instead, "You can't wait any longer. The older you get, the closer you are to hitting the limit."

"Menopause is not a disease, my dear FEN."

"I know. I was being careful not to shock you."

"Shock me."

"Number two: if it's you, the problem can be rectified. Blocked tubes and uterine problems are no longer mysteries to modern medicine. If there is no solution, then you can go for surrogacy. I'll explain...."

"FEN, I went to one of the best schools east of the Niger."

"Okay, Mom; I can do it for you, for us."

"What?"

"Don't worry. It will be your ovum, Daddy's thingy, and we are there. As soon as I drop my pen, we can all go and see the world. A year later, you are back with a child. It will be in the family, and nobody will ever know. Besides, the child will be truly my brother or my sister or, preferably, both."

Chināsa thought about it for some time: "Have you told your Daddy anything of the nature?"

"You think I am stupid or something."

"No, and stop the sarcasm. Don't say anything about this. It may be an abomination where we come from."

"Of course, it is; as is everything they can't explain. When did they stop killing twins? Grandma said her father saw loads thrown into Eziuke *'Evil Forest'* or Sacred Grove—as we now know it. When did they stop severing female clitoris, eh? The town barely spared Grandma's age grade, she told me. Surrogacy will be abomination because a man can choose to have another woman to this day. We don't want to go there; do we, Mom?"

"No!"

"Good. See, it will only take a wink or a little away match to get an *Auntie Concorde* to move in. Think about that, Mom. It has happened elsewhere; it could happen to us. Your usual threats to check out to Uncle Zakky's will only cause more trouble."

"Okay, my dear, you let me worry about that department. Just don't breathe a word to your Daddy, okay?"

"I didn't tell him you were at school to see me."

"He knows?"

"Mrs. Olisa got in touch with him."

"What did the universal busybody hope to achieve?"

"Mom, she was being pragmatic."

"Pantopragmatic more like."

Nnénna did not know what the word meant exactly, but she guessed that 'busybody' was close. "The Principal wanted to make sure you didn't drive straight to the nearest river."

"FEN!"

"Sorry, Mom; just joking." She held Chināsa's arms as if she did not want her to use them. She would not dare; Gilbert would definitely drive her out of the house. Not having a son was bad enough, in her books; getting physical with Nnénna would tantamount to tempting fate. Nobody messed with his Nnénna, nobody.

"Don't joke with suicide. Ever! It's an abomination; at least, it is where we come from."

"You make that sound like we come from the other end of the world. It's flaming Eziuke on Udi Hills."

They laughed and talked about other people's problems and neighbors. Chināsa encouraged her to associate with her mates in the neighborhood, but Nnénna said she did not have the time. The Commissioners' Quarters got new tenants with recent reshuffles and changes in the governor's cabinet. At first, the children acted like demigods. By the time they touched reality, their fathers were out of office. They did not keep in touch thereafter because the perquisites of power that kept them afloat were gone. They crawled back to whence they had crawled out, unless the man stayed long enough to steal substantial sums of backhand money to build a mansion in the Independence Layout.

Chināsa tried to engage her daughter's interest in serious issues of her background. Nnénna knew about her mother's 'illegitimacy'—a concept that did not exist in Igbo sociology. Nnénna could not recall how she got the gist; she just knew. As Chināsa explained the circumstances, it suddenly came as a shock to her that she had never asked her mother for the precise identity of her biological father. She made a mental note to ask her mother soonest.

For a moment, Chināsa dreaded Nnénna asking her for the facts. As if to cover that up, she took up her stepfather's lineage and explained how Grandma met the Northerner in early 1950s along the old Enugu-Onitsha road.

"In those days, good girls did not go talking to total strangers. Grandma was a single mother, so she was not your average 'good girl.' She was growing up before her time. Alhaji Madaki spoke little Igbo and cut-and-nail English. Grandma not only spoke English and Igbo she spoke good Hausa. Madaki stayed on for some time, using our house as a base. By the time he was ready to move on, Grandma was all set to move up north—with him."

"Grandma!"

When Chināsa's mother, Abigail Ezenāgu, left Eziuke for the North, she was pregnant. Nobody was surprised. In fact, they were surprised she waited that long after Chināsa. She was popular with local lads. They knew she was available and that they could get away with the eventual consequence of pregnancy and child upbringing. However, when the rich Northerner rolled into town the year before, the lads trained their wretched and empty barrels elsewhere. Everybody liked the moneyed Muslim and traveling trader. In spite of his faith, the man guzzled palm wine with locals and parted with cash easily.

Chināsa did not go into more details, which she did not have anyway. "I am talking too much?"

"No, Mom, tell me about you: were you as wild?"

"Well, well, the late sixties… early seventies were a different era."

"I know! Your albums make history in black and white. I wonder why you leave them where Daddy sees them."

"FEN, in this house, we keep no secrets. Your Daddy knew all about me before we got married."

Nnénna did not ask any more questions. Nothing else mattered. Madaki was as good a grandfather as she could wish. "Okay, time to 'go and join your husband'!"

Chināsa was so pleased with herself that she kept Gilbert awake all night telling him what a wonderful woman Nnénna had become. He was thrilled. They spent the long weekend like a second honeymoon.

Monday morning at breakfast in the upstairs kitchenette, Chināsa floated the idea of surrogate motherhood.

Gilbert told her not to mention it again in her dreams. "If I needed to sleep with other women, you could line them up from here to Forcados. Also, I don't need a doctor to transfer my sperm, thank you very much."

"That's not what I mean, Giles."

"Chichi, what exactly do you mean?"

"Please, listen: Okay, I guess I took the other way round. What I mean is that it will be the last resort."

"What are you talking about; last resort for what?"

"And why are you shouting?"

"I am sorry. What do you mean by 'last resort'?"

"I am sure you know what I mean. Another option may make the last resort unnecessary," she continued without acknowledging the apology. As far as she was concerned, he could shout at her and bash her, if he cared. Marriage meant that the man, the provider in her case, was in charge. She could kick and scratch but, after analyzing loose nuts and lousy nickels, the man was the master.

"Listen, woman: If Nnénna is the only child you will conceive, carry to term, and deliver without complications, then Nnénna will be the only child I have. I am not going to sleep with another woman to make a baby. I will not enter into any form of ridiculous surrogate arrangement. Do I make myself clear?"

Chināsa did not have to respond. She did not.

What do women want? Gilbert wondered. The problem may be that many men do not understand gender. Every male generation has tried to figure out women without much success. The Igbo ancestors took a hard long look at the situation and simply declared that extensive interaction between men and women should be mostly one-on-one—never as a group—and should be physically limited to the bedroom. The Muslim-Arab culture took it to the limit and decreed seclusion and veil in public.

In Western societies, where feminist movements have made some strides, men still wonder what women want. It got to a point where some psychology egghead declared that men and women are not from the same planet: Women are from Venus; men are from Mars. Photographic exploration of Mars shows there are no men on the planet—just red rocks. Women are not on Venus either. Maybe, just maybe, women left Venus in a spaceship, landed on Mars—planet of men, took all the men, and came down to Earth to create a colossal confusion that God did not intend.

Who knows!

11

CHINĀSA COULD NOT WAIT FOR TRANSCRIPT OF the film before putting Nnénna's suggestions to work. She did not want to watch the childbirth scenes. She had a fear of newborns, a mild form of pediaphobia. She did not go to see newborn babies until they were weaned or, at least, the umbilical cord had fallen off and healed. Her gifts usually made up for her late visits, so her lateness really bothered no one. Besides, newborns are going nowhere soon.

Faith failed Chināsa miserably. She believed that the power of prayers was going to make everything possible; it just needed to connect through the right reverend. Of course, 'the right reverend' depends on how much money one is willing to pledge as weekly tithe. In her case, the power of prayers was decreasing exponentially with the power of money. The parish priests also demanded more money, which Gilbert willingly provided. She was not going to wait any more for their promised miracles.

As soon as Nnénna went back to school for the first term of her final year at Queen's, Chināsa agreed to travel abroad for the first time in years. Gilbert was pleasantly surprised. He asked his secretary to make first-class arrangements from Lagos to London and on to Las Vegas via Los Angeles. He was determined to spoil her, but Chināsa said she will stop in London. She had been to Las Vegas once, and she never wanted to return. It reminded her so much of her past. To her, it was the Sodom and Gomorrah of America, the capital city of sin.

Gilbert left her in London after they had done all the suggested tests at a Harley Street clinic. He proceeded to Taiwan and Hong Kong. On coming back to London a week later, the doctors had the answers: Sperm count was okay, and she was still ovulating—she knew that. Dr. Keith Dearlove explained the problem with a great deal of techno-medical gobbledygook. Gilbert was not impressed.

"What is the solution?" Gilbert asked rather impatiently.

"I'm coming to that," Dr. Dearlove responded. He came to it after impressing the couple with more medical jargons designed to make the exorbitant fee ingestible. "In simple language, we'll have to do artificial insemination."

"At last," Gilbert gasped. "Work out the details and get on with it. Here are all my phone numbers."

"Thank you," Chināsa said as they drove back to North London. "You don't know how relieved I feel right now that we are near to a solution. I hope it is not too much bother."

"It's all right. I am not bothered. If it makes you feel fine by my side... be with me, then it is worth it. Any other positive result is a bonus. Tell me, how did you get the idea? What made you agree to leave those money-sucking, voodoo vampires and the phony spiritual magicians called 'prayer warriors'?"

She told him. Gilbert was so happy he drove back to Oxford Street and bought pleasant presents for Nnénna. Chināsa was in a shopping mood too. She went over to Harrods and selected the best negligees and underwear available, things that a female teenager needed and things she never had the time to buy for Nnénna. She was beginning to value Nnénna. Her daughter's friendship now meant a lot more than the results of the tests. She had cried and regretted neglecting Nnénna in her mad search for a son. She hoped it was not too late to reclaim her daughter, rather than embrace a sister or, worse, a sister-wife.

Gilbert traveled to the United States after parting with enough semen to keep the doctor busy. He flew back home to Nigeria from there. By the time he came back to London for the third time in two months, Chināsa was missing a period in years. It was just a week gone, but there was no guessing. She knew it, and she could not wait to leave London. Dr Dearlove was against it.

"What does he know," Chināsa protested. "I am carrying the boy, not him."

To make sure everything was okay, Gilbert flew in her gynecologist from Enugu to listen to Dr. Dearlove explain the day-by-day checkups and to establish a professional rapport.

Chināsa must be the happiest person aboard the flight to Lagos. Many happy shoppers had come over to spend some of the petrodollars with which the country was awash. Mrs. Chināsa Iké had no need for all the intercontinental shopping sprees. She had shunned many overseas trips offered by her husband. She had a more important shopping target that money presumably could not buy. She traveled at last and got all she wanted: another baby... no, just another pregnancy... a pregnancy for all her detractors to see.

Gilbert stayed back in Lagos, while Chināsa took a local flight to Enugu two days later. The Lagos branch of his business was booming, and the mansion in Victoria Island needed some urgent landscaping to stem the encroaching erosion from raving Atlantic Ocean waves.

Chināsa could not wait to show off how *sick* she was. All the symptoms of pregnancy heard and never felt manifested in her. She carefully confided in her loudmouthed so-called friends and neighbors, who in turn took the news to town. She resumed her social activities. Whenever a mild odor was in the air, she complained loudly. She left events if things began to heat up a wee bit. The calculated attempts to get attention easily got through to whoever wanted to hear.

Nnénna had just finished her mock exams when the pregnancy got into a hitch. Gilbert refused to move her to London. Keith flew in, but it was not necessary. She had eaten something that did not agree with her system. Luckily, she and the baby were okay.

Three months later, O-Level exams kicked off. With her mother healthy, hale, and happy, and her father's overseas trips cancelled, there was little or no worry. Grandma Abigail moved in to be with Chināsa. Her hangers-on and friends were legion. Fanny, now resident in Lagos, flew in and out of Enugu to supply Chināsa's cosmetics, designer dresses, and high-life gossips.

The girls at Queen's forgot all about Nnénna during the examination fever. Now that final exams were over, she was back in the picture to reclaim her pride of place. Exquisitely beautiful, intellectually sound, and with so much material goodies, she was happening.

Enter the last months of high school, her last days at Queen's. Nnénna moved her social life into the overdrive. She decided it was time to know some of her classmates despite their silly ways. She selected a few mates and accompanied them to the sendoff at College of Immaculate Conception in Uwāni section of the city. The next day, boys came flocking into Queen's High as if their reverend-father principal had locked them away for five years.

Since she had no genuine girlfriend, Nnénna surprisingly found the boys to be better company. They loved her, and they talked and bore no malice. She let them borrow and use her gadgets. One after the other, she lost the few selected girlfriends to juvenile jealousy. One introduced her boyfriend to Nnénna; he dumped her the next day. She met another boy at the gate the same day. They had an innocent but brief, animated discussion. His girlfriend saw them, complained, and got the sack.

It was back to square one. The girls ganged up and threw everything at Nnénna. Carla, the senior prefect, inexplicably led the campaign. Those who saw their boyfriends exchange sincere salutations with Nnénna called her ugly names. Those who wished they had the boys around them cussed her.

Nnénna took in the situation and decided that it was not worth worrying. She had no one to tell; Zina had left the school. The boys kept coming to invite her to parties. She agreed and attended one more sendoff at St Patrick's Emene, just by the airport. The rush to request her hand during slow numbers was all it took to start a battle that brought in a squad of police officers to restore order. She had not given anyone an exclusive come-on. The boys simply went ahead to claim the supposedly virgin territory.

The party restarted as if nothing had happened, as if the commotion was a common crack in a party of boneheads. Trouble soon brewed again. The intervention of senior tutors saved the day.

Nnénna could take it no more. She left.

The party practically ended.

Nnénna took her usual stand-by taxi home. She arrived just as her father was rushing her mother to the University of Nigeria Teaching Hospital (UNTH). She asked the senior maid to disembark. She hopped into the car. She held her mother and comforted her in the backseat as her father negotiated the downtown chaotic traffic by the central motor park called Old Park.

It took trying tooting and threats to get the gateman to let them through the metal bar. Once inside, the doctor and some nervous nurses were waiting for them. Gilbert had called her principal physician before leaving home.

Chināsa lost the baby. Gilbert ordered an autopsy and got the news she wanted to hear: It was a boy. He was obviously devastated, but he was relieved that his wife was well.

The final rites were as elaborate as that of a crown prince who lived a full life only to die before formal coronation. Normally, no one outside the family would hear of the loss directly. Of course, the news eventually seeps through the marketplaces and reaches the ears of all and sundry. People express their sympathies, but only those that are close enough to the family pay sympathy visits to express gratitude to God for the mother's survival, never regrets.

"God gives; God also takes," one woman will say.

"We live here; more shall come," another will add.

"We shall know only those that wish to know us."

"Those that want to stay will stay. Those that don't like what they see, or who we are, should stay the hell away from us with their corpse of a body."

"A safe delivery is a sweet victory, but we got a fine deal," a man may philosophize by way of sincere, strong support. "Tomorrow's market always brings a better bargain."

The Igbo do not consider children not carried to full term as members of the community. Stillborn babies and those that did not survive one native week of four days are unnamed. No one stages an elaborate funeral in honor of the stillborn. On the contrary, the custom celebrates survival of the mother because every pregnant woman is at war with many forces. Every family deems the survival of the mother as a great victory because, if a game escapes today, tomorrow is another day of hunting: *Anụ gbalaa taata, echi bụ ntá.*

A week later, Chināsa called London and made another appointment. Gilbert wanted her to give it up because her body might not take it any more. She refused to buy into his thinking. She will have a son, come rain or shine. If it means living in Dr. Dearlove's office for nine solid months and then some, she will do it.

12

TWO WEEKS LATER, QUEEN'S SENDOFF HELD. THE principal had heard that many boys were coming 'to rush' Nnénna. She prepared. First, she based admission strictly on one-to-one invitation. Then she invited a specific number of girls from Union Girls and the same number from College of Immaculate Conception (CIC). Senior Prefect Carla wanted Federal Government College, Enugu (FGC). Her mother, the principal, obliged her. Being a mixed secondary school, the one-girl-to-one-boy calculation held for FGC.

It was Carla's day. She did not want to share the limelight with anyone. As the outgoing senior prefect and with a direct line to the pinnacle of power, she handpicked her successor. The new SP went out of her way to show her gratitude. Every speech started and ended with "the remarkable reign of wonderful Carla Olisa, our principal's darling daughter," as if anybody needed the reminder. Prizes galore followed. Carla's boyfriend escorted her to and from the podium. Applauses accompanied them.

Nnénna walked up to collect the Library Prefect plaque. The hall came to a standstill. "Thank you very much," she said, "*Merci beaucoup*." A thunderous applause erupted and endured. She walked back up the podium to acknowledge the applause. She set off more applause until hands reddened.

Nnénna walked down the dais. Carla was visibly vexed. Her boyfriend was so captivated she had to elbow him to stop grinning like a beach bum. Of course, Carla could parade a boyfriend openly because her mother is not Igbo; otherwise, she would not have had the nerve or the chutzpah to identify with a boy so openly.

The principal and staff left after the presentations, light refreshments, and opening of the dance floor. Some junior teachers stayed back to keep an eye on the goings-on without interfering with the program.

Nnénna was circulating and dancing. Every time she looked around, she noticed the gawking eyes of Carla's boyfriend trained on her. Carla saw him and rebuked him, again. He apologized but, as soon as Carla went to order fellow students around, he turned and looked at Nnénna.

A boy Nnénna knew from previous parties came for a dance. She obliged him. She normally did not refuse to dance. At the same time, she did not hang around anybody for too long. Thus, she avoided any territorial claims that marred the last party at St Patrick's College. She kept moving to avoid queues and jostling for vantage position around her.

Nnénna knew Frank Obi-Nwaeze, Carla's boyfriend. He was a first-year student of law at the Enugu Campus of University of Nigeria (UNEC). Carla's twin brother, Carl, was his friend. Both were ex-CIC academic stars, and both were presently at UNEC. Frank was a handsome boy. Tall, well built, and with a baby face, he was one person that never had to run after girls; he ran from them. Carla had an edge: They moved in the same social circle; in fact, both families were neighbors. Frank's father was the State's chief judge; Carla's father was the chief medical officer.

Carl showed interest in Nnénna, but Carla appeared and took him to the girls she had lined up for him. He was not interested in any of the chosen chicks. Carl had seen Nnénna before, and he had not stopped hoping to hit the bull's eye with a disarming smile. He told Frank to keep Carla off his back, but Frank flashed a schemer's smug smile. Asked if he was interested, Frank said he and Nnénna had a mutual acquaintance: Zina.

"You reckon I'll crash?" Carl wanted to know.

"It's hard to say. Moses did strike water out of stone. No harm in trying."

Carl was making some progress with Nnénna when bossy sister Carla showed up again. "Carl, Frank wants a word. Now! Hello, Finlay, how are you? Nice dress."

"Es Pee. Ah, so you managed to tear yourself away from the eighth wonder of the modern world?"

"A wonder your sticky hands can never get to touch. Anyway, some of the girls are complaining about you."

"Why?" Nnénna was visibly surprised.

"Come on, Finlay, go and get yourself a boyfriend and stop messing around with theirs."

Nnénna smiled. "If you had not sent Carl back to those village pumpkins you were grooming for him, maybe, just maybe, your problem could have been halved. Okay, since they cannot fight their wars, why not continue championing their causes by telling them how you keep yours obedient?"

"You must be crazy, you know. Why would I do that? You think my Frankie fancies Finlay? Keep on dreaming." Carla walked away toward Frank.

Nnénna looked up and saw Frank looking again in her direction, but Carla was in his line of observation. He smiled. Nnénna winked. He winked back. Carla smiled, walked into his arms, gave him a peck, and walked on. The busybody wanted to be everywhere at the same time.

Carl found his way back to Nnénna. He felt and acted like the top dog. So-called 'senior boys' respected his space. Carl was notorious for seducing girls in record time, so the boys walked past casually and wished him good luck with Nnénna by slapping his back. Closer friends offered handshakes. He was accepting one of such special handshakes that ended with a flip of the fingers and a 'ride-on' call when Nnénna made her move. She had a plan to execute. Carl was no longer a part of it.

"Excuse me, Carl. I shall see you later."

Nnénna walked up to the DJ and requested *Sexual Healing* by Marvin Gaye. It was still the hottest blues in town; DJs normally reserved the number until everybody had paired and loosened up a bit. All the boys went across the floor like a swarm of swallow birds asking the girls they had fancied all evening to dance. Carla tried to make her way back to her boyfriend, but twinned bodies, heaving bosoms, and wriggling bums made passing through the dancing floor almost impossible. An old flame held her, told her to stop trying to get across, and took her to dance.

Frank saw Nnénna as she warded off requests to dance and winked again. She winked back, smiled, and left the hall.

As if a dog determined to sniff out a bitch on heat, Frank followed. Nnénna walked toward the dormitories, looked back, and saw him. She walked on and turned right toward her dormitory. It was not yet dark, but the sun had lost its luster. Frank followed her.

Half an hour later, Carla was reasonably furious. Frank was missing. Nothing else mattered. She could hardly control her emotions. When she realized that Nnénna was missing too and that Carl was not with her, she was flaming furious.

At times, human beings are better off leaving certain things alone to play out because those things are destined to happen. They must happen for undesired events to fold. Unnecessary provocation triggers unneeded sequence of events to unfold and hold.

Carla called up seven big girls and asked them to follow her. They did. It was a terrible mistake. The unintended mistake marked an intersection of destinies, the destinies of those directly concerned. For her thoughtless quest to win at all cost, their lives took a sharp turn to their destinies.

13

SHE HAD DECIDED A LONG TIME BEFORE THE DAY that she wanted to graduate into womanhood on the day she graduated from high school. Nnénna dreamt about it the night before, and she knew there was no putting it off. She had no one yet to cut the ribbon. She did not have a boyfriend. Carl was her number one at a point, but Carla chose to tell him how to behave. Then she decided to expand the agenda and use it to cut Carla's ego down to size. Carl still fitted the bill, but something told her to be bolder, to hit harder and below the bellybutton.

"Some junior girls saw Finlay and Frank going in the direction of the dormitories," a smallish student informed Carla. Others said they went toward the classroom block through a shortcut route known as 'Apian Way.' Carla and her hooters trudged on toward the building. A handful of excited junior girls followed, but Carla's head-hen warned them away with threats of corporal punishment. Carla and company approached each classroom carefully, peeping through keyholes or windows with loose louver blades.

They came to the far-end classroom. Its windows had lost more louver blades than they had on, so no one bothered to lock the door. In the middle of the room, Frank and Nnénna were on top of a row of desks coupled to form a concave cot. Nnénna had made up a love cradle with her beddings, which she picked up from the dormitory on their way from the hall. The senior prefect stopped. Her friends froze. They were all seeing such an act live for the first time. Some of them must have done it in the darkness of night, but none had ever seen it done at dusk.

The girls watched Frank and Nnénna as they did justice to foreplay as if they had planned and rehearsed it. Then they got down to the real deal.

Only heavens knew what books she had been reading, or what X-rated videotapes her father mistakenly brought home from Amsterdam, Holland. The feelings Nnénna lent voice were celestial symphony to Frank's ear. He was flying away regardless of gravity, but Nnénna held him. Her manicured fingers grasped his bare back as his mouth explored all her facial curves. She held one leg up in air; the other laced on his bare behind. Frank groaned as he tried to get into her. He was putting in considerable effort, as if searching for something valuable, something he dared not touch. His hands moved all over her body, resting often on her baby-soft boobs. She twitched as the pain of his thrust hit her. To avoid physical harm, she tightened her pelvic muscles and summoned sanguine support from her brain to the distressed district.

"Are you hurting?" he asked with considerable affection tainted with unsteady respiratory acoustics. "Are you...?" Frank repeated without stopping.

"A little... yes." Nnénna showed some signs of discomfort.

"Do you want me to stop?" Frank asked.

"No, no, go ahead. Just take it easy ... yes, easy."

Frank complied and stopped trying to gain full entry. He kissed her on the mouth. The moist softness of her lips sent shivers down his body. He stuck out his tongue expecting a little resistance. Nnénna let his tongue into her mouth like a hot tungsten knife through butter and did many things to it. He did not know there was more to his tongue than just a primary sensor for salt and pepper.

Frank was so excited his hip went to Katanga; hers, to Kigali. They established a rhythm of reciprocating downward and upward movement, oh-ing and ah-ing in crescendo until something took over their beings.

Oh, oh, he let out; ah, ah, she complemented.

In the excitement that followed the final blitz, Frank lost the rhythm. Nnénna was in control. She tightened the hold of her legs. Lo and behold, right there and then, he experienced something fascinating, something he had read about in books; something Carla had promised but never delivered, and something other boys boosted and bragged about the many times and positions possible and impossible. He had labeled the many stories empty and obviously false. He now knew better, but he could never share this experience for a million dollars. He swore to keep it to himself and cherish it.

Frank exhaled and then smiled. Geneva, at last, and there was peace in their time. Nnénna gave Frank a funny look. Then she smiled to reassure him that everything was okay. She felt something too. She felt something she knew existed… something she had not intended to feel. She was out to muck around but found herself liking him and loving it.

"Are you okay?" she asked.

He nodded shyly, wanting to cover his face. Nnénna was surprised that Frank was not as knowledgeable as she had imagined. She knew he wanted to get up and put on his pants. Either he did not want her to see his spent manhood or he did not know how to handle post-coitus protocol. Nnénna had no experience either, but she had read the love theories as espoused in Kama Sutra. She had read that some egghead called it pangs of guilt or post-coitus mea culpa. Whatever it was, Frank's face wore all the signs. She kept him there like an amateur sadist, wondering what he was doing with Carla these past months.

From across the room, the stupefied spectators looked at each other. They were dumbfounded. Carla was so upset she began to sob. The girls held her, shaking her to prevent her from crying out.

Carla coughed.

Frank froze. Nnénna frowned. They looked up from their dreamland and saw reality. She had forgotten about getting even and drifted to enjoying herself with abandon. He took one look at Carla's face and got the message. He tried to get off Nnénna, jump down from the desk, and grab his pants.

"Relax, Frankie," Nnénna said sweetly and loud enough for Carla's auricular consumption. She was incredibly calm, collected, and callous. He was anxious and flighty. "I said to take it easy, okay?"

Frank was nonplussed. Slowly, Nnénna let one leg drop; then she let the other leg drop casually with a deliberate slow motion. He pulled away, jumped down, grabbed his pants, and ran out through the back window like a rocket fired off NASA's Cape Canaveral.

"Come back here, Frankie," Carla yelled, "Come here, you yellow rat!"

Only the wetness of his unrestrained manhood kept his acceleration in check. Carla ran after him. The girls followed. Frank jumped the fence and ran into the farms in the neighboring UNEC grounds.

They came to a sudden stop at the fence. "Senior, it is of no use," a member of her posse counseled.

"I will deal with him; trust me," Carla vowed as they marched back and entered the classroom to confront Nnénna. "After dealing with the bloody idiot with no intelligence, he will never look for my trouble."

"Intelligence is what an idiot lacks," Nnénna wisecracked. She was taking her time ever so slowly. She did not rush to clean nor gather her clothes in a hurry. She simply stood up, pulled up her panties, and put on her dress. The 100 percent silk, summer-perfect, beach-colors outfit was not rumpled. She expected no bloodstains, albeit her first time. She had made sure no man was going to see her bleed in the name of losing virginity. She smiled and felt good about the decision.

Losing virginity was not something she wished to share. The trauma of her first menstrual period was so embarrassing her father took her to a specialist gynecologist who got rid of her hymen surgically, since it has no anatomical function, as the doctor explained, and suppressed her painful periods hormonally. She knew then that medicine was not for her.

Nnénna did not run from paper tigers like Carla and her band of bootlickers. They thought Nnénna had run away to pack her things and get ready to flee from the dorm. She simply switched back to her original plan, as if what they had seen were scenes for a home movie. She stepped forward to the stunned students who were waiting for Carla to make up her mind on what next to do.

Not one of them spoke as Nnénna approached. They moved to allow Carla her normal center-rank position. Some wiped their eyes symbolically. Nnénna flashed a sly and satisfactory smile devoid of any feeling of remorse. The girls made way for Nnénna as if she were inspecting a guard of honor for an extraordinary performance.

Carla stood her ground, ready for physical confrontation. Nnénna will trash her in a fair fight, but Carla would sink her teeth into her opponent's chest and hope her opponent would not be courageous enough to bite back. Separation squad would move in, and she would claim victory—a vain victory that would take away a chunk of her hurt and humiliation.

With her shoes swinging in her left hand, Nnénna still stood taller than Carla, who was not short by any standard. Right hand on her waist and eyes skewed, she looked Carla over and continued her approach. Other senior girls closed in from behind her as she walked past them.

Nnénna looked over her shoulders menacingly. The girls stopped. She stopped and cast a what-next look in Carla's direction. "Got something to say?"

"Have you no shame?" Carla blurted.

"Shame? Hmm, let me see: How do you spell 'shame'?" Nnénna was making fun of Carla's poor spelling skills, which teachers ignored because her mother was their boss.

"You look at my boyfriend again, I'll deal with you."

"You can have him back; I've finished," she snorted and snapped her fingers lackadaisically as she sidestepped Carla.

Nnénna walked across the small grass forecourt where the national flag flew as if in salute of her triumph or in mourning for the loss of her innocence. The girls followed her like Swedish sheep and Gambian goats let loose in the woods.

"Slut," Carla yelled. It did not register with the girls; they were hearing the word for the first time.

Nnénna ignored Carla. She suddenly turned onto a dirt road to the dorms, hoping that Carla's passing psychosis will steer her on a straight path back to the hall.

"Whore!" The girls looked unmoved and followed Carla and her bulging rage. "Hopeless hole! Presidential prostitute! *Akwụnakwụna! Shara! Waka-waka!*" These terms brought home her yelling and heckling. Carla continued: "Hotel Harlot!" Nnénna walked on. "*Ashawo* bastard!"

Nnénna stopped. She could take irate and older Carla calling her a streetwalker in any language and in any dialect or slang, but not a bastard. She turned. Carla stopped, and the posse stood still. She looked Carla straight in the face. She saw pain in her dull-green eyes. Carla was down and out; kicking her was unnecessary. "Go get a life," she said, sighed sympathetically, and walked toward the hall.

"Finlay, I say you are a cheap lay."

"*C'est ne pas* cheap, Carla," she retorted. "Ask Frankie: 'Fine lay' is more like it." She allowed herself a little grin, stopped briefly, and walked on without looking back.

The girls grinned and murmured their appreciation of the aptness of her unstudied wit. Carla did not get it; she was too tight to think, too hurt to heal.

Others approached as the group walked back to the hall. Some students holding hands or kissing disengaged as they recognized Carla and her posse. Carla was still the mighty SP, but she was not interested in controlling anyone; her house was on fire, and she could not afford the folly of chasing rats. Carla soon realized she had to recourse to damage limitation. Having hushed others to keep quiet about the incident, she tried to act normal. It was obvious she did not intend to lose Frank to Nnénna; that would be the deepest dent.

A Rembrandt-red Mercedes drove up from the gate. Nnénna turned and saw Carla and the other girls looking at the car as it cruised up the dusty road. She stopped. Carla's posse stopped too. The Munich machine in all its majesty stopped before her like a remote-controlled robotic pet. A chauffeur dressed in navy-like attire with a cap to match came out, saluted, and opened the owner's corner.

"Don't be ridiculous, Nicholas. Why are you opening the door for me? My box is in the dorm and, as you can see, the party is still on," Nnénna said, raising her voice and sounding happy. Other girls milled around. Shorter students stretched or knelt to catch a glimpse.

"Ọga said you might need a lift home...."

"Ọga? I don't have a boss."

"Oh, I am sorry, Miss Nnénna. Your Papa said...."

"Good. Any of you girls want a ride into town?" Nobody spoke. She looked at Carla and wanted to say that she was sorry, but she decided not to make her day. Instead, she said to the senior girls present, "A vehicle will be picking up my things tomorrow at about 10 AM. I'll welcome anyone who wants a ride home or to Motor Park." She turned to the driver: "The keys, Nicholas."

As Nnénna drove away, one girl shook her head as if shaking off her state of unconsciousness and asked no one in particular, "Is this girl a ghost or an angel in human flesh?"

"Like her magic-leg mother, she is a water witch," another girl declared with an I-should-know tone.

"You know them?" Carla asked.

"Yes. We are from the same hometown. She is definitely emerging as everybody expected: an original *ogbanje* from the bottom of deep sea."

Carla piloted the informer away from other students.

She went on: "Her mother is an only child... before her own mother married one Hausa man. Nnénna is again an only child. You know how they behave: It's either they go back young to be born again, or they block the womb."

Girls who are *ogbanje* belong to the world of the living and of the dead. They have the power to go and to come... the predisposition to die young, but it is not infectious.

Carla was not in a balanced mood. She encouraged the silly spin. The other girls were uninterested. Just by driving the car away, Nnénna bought and sold them. The next day, they will be gone. Some students had already moved out of the dorm, and not a few jostled to hitch a ride in the minibus coming to pick Nnénna's bedding and review notes stuffed into a pretty portmanteau.

Carla did not want the story of what happened with Frank to get out. For her own sake, she was ready to let the story die; for her pride, she was tempted to turn every stone until she extracted her pound of flesh.

Love is a passing psychosis, a phase of deep psychological distraction, or a momentary mental mess of varying duration. Since all stages in sanity-insanity spectrum affect different people differently, different people react to love lunacy differently. Carla decided to use the stories from the informer to scare Frank out of his wits and to make him dream no more of the girl they called Finlay. Like the lunatic who set fire to his family house and declared elatedly that he had created an open space, she succeeded in derailing her destiny.

14

NNÉNNA STEPPED OUT OF THE BENZ AND ASKED Nicholas to park the car. She walked straight to her room. Gilbert was on the balcony with his wife. The way Nnénna walked with her shoes in her hand, he suspected something was wrong. When five minutes later she still had not come to give him a hug, his suspicion deepened. Chināsa noticed his unease.

Half an hour later, they went to check on her. She was in the bathroom. The strong smell of bubbles of passion fruit oozed out with the steam from a hot bath.

"Mommy, are you all right?"

"Yes, Daddy," Nnénna responded instantly.

"FEN, add a little water to the foam bath, please!"

"I'm sorry, Mom. I'll buy you another bottle."

"That particular brand is organic. It is imported."

"Knock it off, Chichi," Gilbert intervened.

"Don't tell me that, Giles. Fanny walked the length and breadth of Oxford Street, London twice before she found just a dozen tubes at the other end of Baker Street."

Gilbert was not amused. He walked into his studio and fixed a drink. He was sure something was wrong. He knew her daughter very well; they were that close.

They finished supper in silence.

"I'm going to bed," Nnénna declared with no emotions.

"Good night, my dear." He hardly ate a morsel.

"Good night, Daddy. Night, night, Mom."

"Sleep tight, FEN."

Husband and wife exchanged quick glances and watched as their daughter glided upstairs as if she was sleepwalking.

Gilbert's noticeable concern amused his wife. It was the first time Nnénna went to bed without hugging her father. She had not hugged her mother since the day they disagreed over the juvenile Erico Angels' poem. Chināsa smiled and stopped short of laughing out loudly when Gilbert frowned with an undisguised reproach.

"I'm sorry, darling," she said, "but she's leaving the nest."

"Something is troubling her and you can't see it?" He got up, wiped his mouth needlessly and flung the hand towel across the table. He walked up to Nnénna's room and tapped gently on the door.

"Who is it?" she asked with an aloof tone.

"Mommy love, it's me. Are you awake?"

She was. He eased himself in. She was sitting on the bed, her hand across her knee. Gilbert sat by the foot of the bed. She recoiled, straining herself not to make it apparent that she wanted no physical contact.

"I'm sorry. I had a lousy day, but I am okay."

"Anything I should know?"

"Nothing I can't handle."

"You will tell me if you are in any trouble at all?"

"I promise. On Grandma's grave," she swore.

That was very touching. Gilbert got up and walked to the door to hide his steamy eyes. "Sweet dreams."

"Daddy?" she called out. He stopped. "I love you."

He turned back, pulled the quilt over her, and patted her on the shoulder. He turned on the bedside lamp, turned off the ceiling lights, and walked out.

Nnénna sat up, wondering whether it was worth it. She felt like she had known Frank in another world. She would do it again, with or without Carla's provocation. She felt good about it. Strangely, she felt a huge pang of guilt stabbing her heart's core for being unfaithful, not to her *Chi* but to another man—her father.

Suddenly, she startled and said audibly, "He is my father, damn it!" She smiled to reassure herself that she was sane. She drove herself into deep thoughts about the meaning and nature of sex. She was now a woman, she assured herself, and she intended to act like one.

Reverend Father Eze, who had re-baptized her a Catholic, was to say a graduation mass for her the next day. By the time she woke up, her parents had come back from the special Sunday service. She went to the kitchenette for a glass of juice. Her mother was there, working on a new cake recipe.

Nnénna expressed her regrets to her mother, who in turn assured her that Father Eze, her father's best friend from high school, understood. She had bigger problems on her plate: Her thoughts about her feelings for Frank she could contain by escaping to London, but how to handle her father was a thorny issue. It took a lot of courage to decide on the next move. She walked across the living room and quietly eased herself into the studio.

"Mind if I disturb you, sir," she said lightheartedly.

Gilbert looked up from the books he was doing. He got up and walked toward her with arms spread. She walked into him, buried her head on his shoulders, and tried to open her lachrymal taps, but she could not cry. "It's all right, love; please don't think about it."

Reassured that nothing had changed, she started by saying: "I have done something silly, something I should have left for later... something I should not have done, something I do not want to call by its natural name."

"What might that be like, Mommy?"

"It is embarrassing."

"You don't have to tell me. You did whatever you did. You are alive. We will deal with the feelings."

"It's not that simple. I feel like I have hurt you in some kind of stupid way. I really can't explain the strange feeling."

"Then don't. Let me guess: You did whatever you did, I am guessing, thinking that it is okay... or you would not have done it. You liked it, presumably, but you now have a little remorse. Listen: It is your life. Do not mind what people say. What did I tell you last Christmas?"

"Let me see. Oh, I remember: 'Whatever you do in this world should be done to benefit self first, humanity second. The first law of nature is self-preservation or the conservation of species.' Or something like that?"

"That's another way of putting it. So, relax."

Nnénna knew then that he had figured it out. She gave him the outline using the Biblical forbidden fruit.

"Anybody I know... someone your age?"

"Obi-Nwaeze," she divulged.

"The Judge... Francis Obi Nwaeze?"

"No! His son, Frank Obi-Nwaeze."

"Well, well, well. What a small world."

"What do you mean?"

"It's a long story. Do you want to get away early?" She nodded. "You're booked for the last flight. I shall call Lagos and have the driver pick you up."

She nodded again and wondered why she ever doubted his love and friendship. "I am sorry," she mumbled.

"Hey, it's okay. *C'est la vie*, the French say. You do not have to be sorry about whatever transpired. You wanted it, you did it... life goes on."

"Daddy, it is not that simple," Nnénna said as she reached for the doorknob.

"Come back here, please."

Nnénna walked back and stood some distance, her eyes lowered more in guilt than in respect. "Yes, Daddy."

"Sit down, please."

She complied. To lighten the situation, she said, "Should I fasten the seatbelt?"

"No, no," Gilbert assured her. "This is just an aside. I am not too crazy about romantic love, but I know it exists. I do not know what it is; I cannot define it if my life depends on defining it. This much I must tell you: You cannot share romantic love; it is indivisible. Once you are sure of this young man, feel free to express yourself and give it your best while it lasts."

"How?" she asked directly and looked up.

"I wish I know, my dear; I wish I know the answer. Based on my own life experiences, you cannot hide something that good, a feeling so sacred and sweet. The Bible tells us not to hide light. You cannot hide light. Light illuminates darkness. Love is light; hide it and it could set off an eventual inferno."

"Thank you, Daddy."

"I should thank you for trusting me. You will get used to the difficulties of love. Love is a personal experience, and no two are the same. You want me to hint your mother and soften the ground a bit?"

She shook her head and said almost to herself, "I really did not mean to go this far, and I must have hurt more than a few persons in the process."

Gilbert ignored the confession. Asking her for the details was unnecessary. He preferred to give her the space needed to come to terms with losing her virginity and telling her father about it. "Go get some rest."

Nnénna walked toward the door, stopped and, without turning, she said, "Daddy, I guess you know now why I was lousy last night?"

"Yep, but you should not feel that way. It does not make you dirty. Hey?" he called out as she went for the doorknob. "Next time, do take necessary precautions."

"There won't be a next time, Daddy; it's a promise. Once is enough, believe me."

"I do, Mommy; I do." The statement shocked Gilbert, but he smiled. "Just take your time."

"I said once... one man is enough."

"My dear, we are not God."

"He gave us brains to use."

"I agree, and we must use them."

Nnénna turned round to face her father. "Thank you, Daddy; you are very understanding."

Gilbert thought of his mother and prayed to God not to allow a repeat of the past: She is still young, and she will definitely get over the first-time shock. He did not want details of the encounter.

Chināsa was ready to roll. She was looking forward to a repeat of the artificial insemination. Dr. Dearlove still had some stock of her husband's semen, so his presence was not necessary. Nnénna needed nothing special; she had her papers. Her school daughter had retrieved and returned all her stuff from boarding school. She was set to leave town.

After lunch, they called the local airport to confirm, but Nigerian Airways had cancelled the last flight to Lagos. The Monday morning first flight will be on first-come basis. They relaxed to enjoy a quiet Sunday afternoon.

Nnénna was feeling her old self again. She stayed home and watched *Matlock* repeats. There was not much to do. She never shopped, and she had no girlfriend in town. She hated girlie gossips and chitty-chatty talks about boys. She was not good at writing love letters, though she got loads of them from boys she had met at debating conferences. The letters amused her, but she found them distracting. Though she read them all, she dutifully destroyed and discarded them, noting no names or addresses.

15

THEY WERE EATING DINNER. THE PHONE RANG. It was for Nnénna. She did not want to take any calls. Her father mouthed who it was. She rushed to him and wrenched the cordless receiver off his hand.

"I have been calling your private line all day," the caller stated, sounding relieved.

"Zina de Chick, what's new and different, girl?"

"Nné, we need to talk. Please, please, I really need your help. I feel like I have blown my life away. I am lost, lost like a goat without a herder, a canoe on high seas, and I am supposed to be my parent's precious pearl that cannot be lost in a sack of Sapele stones."

Nnénna walked up to her room. Zina opened up and let out as much as was possible to convince Nnénna that she needed immediate help.

Zina had crowned her secondary school career a year earlier with an unassailable record of perfect distinction in West African School Certificate (WASC) examinations. She went to Federal Government College for her A-Level courses. It was not necessary, but her father believed in doing things 'the good old British way.' She excelled in the three courses. Her father told her to take a year off and see the world. Thereafter, she could choose any university in Britain for her undergraduate studies. The course was not debatable: law.

She took the offer and left town just before Nnénna's final exams in May. The last time Nnénna spoke with her, she was to attend the lavish 18th birthday party of Tee Jay, the spoilt son of a corrupt, fugitive political powerhouse named Alhaji Tijani Jibril Dangoya.

Tony Ikpeama, Zina's father, was arguing Dangoya's case in Lagos, taking out injunctions in as many courts as listened. In Britain, top English lawyers applied their legal might in fighting Nigeria's extradition requests.

"Zina…," Nnénna interjected as the monologue became winding without much substance, "I will see you on Tuesday. We shall talk. Whatever it is, we shall resolve it. So how did the party go?"

"It was okay, except that Tee Jay paraded me around all night and relegated Consolatta to the background."

"No, you didn't do that to her," Nnénna protested. Consolatta was Zina's best friend and Tee Jay's girlfriend.

"I thought he was just being nice. The attention was … well, seductive, and it helped the admission of the custom-made *Tee Jay Champagne* through what he called my 'gazelle-like throat'."

"What happened next? Come on, let go of the gist, girl."

Zina gave her the synopsis. Tee Jay took her home. In the morning, she got her bearing easily: She was in her room. She brought down her left leg, inexplicably placed on a man. Then she felt the wetness of him in her. The feeling of a strange substance that did not belong down there in her person was chilling.

"Oh my God," Nnénna exhaled noisily.

"That was exactly my reaction, girl. Tee Jay murmured something and went back to sleep. I got up and began the arduous task of trying to unscramble the omelet. The guilt hung in there like a dart driven into pulp. I was disgusted with myself. I felt like crying… no, screaming. I felt cheap and cheapened, cheated and chaffed."

"Okay, but that was almost two months. Get over it, girl," Nnénna giggled. "These things often happen."

"I wish it was that easy."

"You're in love?"

Zina had no bona-fide boyfriend in high school. Frank was the closest boy in her life, but it was platonic. She never went to social outings more risqué than her birthday parties. She did not attend her Queen's sendoff, the equivalent of American high school prom. One week in London, she was consuming choice champagne and luring lovers to bed.

"So what is the problem?" Nnénna probed.

Zina told her. Six weeks after the night that should not have happened, she still waited for her painful period to come and go before she confirmed her flight to Boston, USA. "I am still waiting. I am going insane here."

"Calm down, girl," Nnénna counseled like an aunt talking to a naughty-but-nice niece. "Listen: as I have told you, I'll be with you by Tuesday morning."

"God bless you, my dear."

"Whatever you're feeling, sleep over it. Catch up on the latest film releases and get some rest; you'll need it."

"Nné-o, I will be counting the seconds."

"Be my guest, but don't go counting sheep… court sleep."

Flight BA 074 took off on schedule. Nnénna slept through the six-hour flight. Chināsa could never go to sleep in a plane if she flew nonstop from Heathrow to Hong Kong. The fact that she achieved nothing by watching others sleep had not changed her mindset. In her book, if God Almighty had wanted humans to fly, he would have given them wings.

Nnénna woke up as the cabin crew began to collect plastic cups and sundry junks, making sure passengers fastened their seatbelts. She had a lot on her mind. She cast her mind back to Enugu. The flight to Lagos in a noisy Nigerian Airways jet was boring. It had to stop in Benin City to allow some military aircrafts to land at the local airport in Lagos. The 45-minute flight took two hours. They had the whole day to spend at their new mansion on Victory Island before heading to Murtala Muhammed International Airport, Lagos.

"Ladies and Gentlemen, this is Captain Rose Brown."

"A woman?" Chinasa whispered to Nnénna. Whether it was sincere admiration or discomfort with a female pilot, Nnénna did not ask. She was more interested in getting off the flying metallic contraption.

The captain continued: "We are starting our initial descent into London Gatwick. The temperature on the ground is normal for this time of the year... overcast skies with light rain. We shall have you on the ground in about eh...m twenty minutes, that will be about ten minutes earlier than expected, but I'm sure we will have no problem docking. We thank you once again for flying with us, and we hope to see you in the near future on one of our flights."

The television switched off. The flight data still displayed. The plane whooshed and whined across patches of clouds. Nnénna looked out of the window. The early morning lights of London City were very visible and serene. She closed the window before her mother reminded her. Chināsa was always nervous on taking off and landing. On the other hand, Nnénna found turbulence difficult to handle; consequently, she slept through most long flights.

"Flight attendants, please prepare for arrival."

They landed, disembarked, and moved to immigration and customs formalities at London Gatwick.

"For how long *arr* you staying?" a Sikh immigration officer asked.

"For as long as we like, Mr. Singh," Nnénna snapped.

"Will you stop and let me do this, Mighty Madam," Chināsa growled like a lioness. The man on duty at the Immigration post took no notice of the impatient teenager who was anxious to get into town. "We are here on vacation. We are regular visitors. We have a home in London."

"I see. Welcome back home then, and enjoy your stay. You too, Miss Finlay... nice name."

In a cab to their house located in the same North London suburb as the Ikpeama's, Chināsa asked Nnénna why she was in a foul mood, judging by the way she talked to the Sikh immigration officer.

"It's none of his business, is it? For how long did he state he was staying when he came?"

"FEN, I've never seen you so rude to total strangers. The customs officer was as polite as can be."

"Polite? What a polite thing to say: 'Are you carrying any illegal substances?' I would tell him if I had illegal drugs, right! There is a limit to polite insults one can take."

"Well, Miss Mighty Giles, when you go to someone's house, you knock politely, wipe your feet, wait to be invited in, and wait to be told to sit down. Okay?"

Nnénna looked in the driver's rearview mirror and caught his eyes. He smiled. She frowned and chided him: "Please watch the road, mister." The driver complied.

Nnénna was on the phone to Zina as soon as they walked into their house.

Chināsa inspected the house. The caretaker had cleaned and made needed repairs. She had not slept a wink since they left Lagos for London. She needed to sleep. She was not used to worrying about Nnénna in Enugu because she rarely went anywhere; in London, there was no basis for anxiety.

"Take some money from my purse for taxi fare," she remembered to say before Nnénna left the house for Zina's.

"How much, Mom?"

"Do I look like a black cab driver? Take four or five tens... pounds; the naira notes won't get you far here."

Nnénna grimaced as she looked into the purse. It was not the amount of cool cash her mother carried but the shocking realization that she had never touched money. At Queen's, the principal had a standing fund for all her needs, and she never needed to buy anything.

Zina briefed Nnénna on the one-night stand. Nnénna took some time to take it in before laying out the plans. It was as if she was the one in Zina's situation. She did not go into the blame game, which Zina dreaded. Nnénna did not know exactly how best to handle the situation, but Zina saw that she cared, that she wanted to help her, be with her, and share the curse and or cross of Eve.

Much later, Nnénna phoned her mother to announce a delayed return. Her mother did not mind if she slept over. A friend was visiting from Camberwell, and they planned to be out of the house until ten that night or thereabouts.

The girls mapped out the strategies. There was no getting away from telling Zina's parents. Unlike Nnénna, Zina was equally close to her parents. Eight o'clock, Zina called her mother in Enugu, told her that she was not feeling well, and she needed her to come over to London earlier than planned. Zina's mother needed no convincing; she knew all about her child's gynecological problems. She had nursed her every month since the first episode, and there was little relief from doctors. One of the best gynecologists in town said that her first pregnancy should stop the symptoms.

It just did.

16

TONY IKPEAMA WAS SURPRISED TO SEE HIS OLD friend, Mr. Justice Francis Obi Nwaeze, visit without warning so early on a workday. Since Tony dispatched him to the bench, following the early 1970s State vs. Iké case, their friendship had cooled considerably. They met in 1960s Britain during their undergraduate years. The popular opposition to British involvement in the Nigeria-Biafra War brought them together. Called to the bar on the same day and in the same city of London, they became friends.

Soon after the cessation of hostilities, they headed home with young families to help in rebuilding their devastated region. Nwaeze took the softer state civil service option. Tony chose the uncharted waters of postwar private practice. The State v. Iké case provided his first big break.

Nwaeze wanted to prove that he could nail the big boys, but he picked on the wrong person. Tony was livid when he detected serious irregularities showing that someone was waging a private war because Gilbert had refused to sell a piece of land by Presidential Hotel.

Nwaeze knew about the secret vendetta, hid the facts, and refused to release the pertinent papers when the judge so demanded. The no-nonsense judge did not hide his anger. On his way to begin a week of confinement for contempt of court, the governor pardoned Obi Nwaeze. The next week, he moved to the bench. An unabashed government loyalist, military governors found him dependable in deciding tacky and tricky cases to favor the state. It was no surprise that a military governor promoted him over his superiors and contemporaries to the top of state judiciary hierarchy.

"Tony, this is not a social visit," Nwaeze said after the hand-washing rituals and kolanut communion. He proceeded to tell Tony Ikpeama the full story.

"Obi, you are staring at a nasty case that could tear up our circle," Tony said. "Let me get this straight: Mrs. Olisa put it in writing to the Dean of Law and threatened legal action?" Nwaeze nodded. "What did Bernard say?"

"You know Dr. Bernard Olisa and his strange sense of straightjacket German justice."

"No, there is more to it; even expatriate wives know that those who sow wind in this town reap tornadoes."

"Well, I guess Frankie and Carla...."

"Ah ha, and we agreed that our children will marry each other. If you break it, you will pay me. Let me see: £1000.00 in 1969 is now worth... what?"

"Tony, this is serious, please. I'm going to fight this if it is the last thing I do," Nwaeze declared.

"Okay, let me have the documents."

Nwaeze gave him copies of signed and notarized witness accounts, letters, and copies of handwritten confessions.

Suddenly, Tony got up. "You want to fight? You have a fight. If Gilbert cries foul, Frank is going to jail."

"What? Finlay is Gilbert Iké's daughter?"

"The one and only daughter of Mighty Giles," Tony said without batting an eyelid. "Names like Zina, Finlay, Carla, Amanda, and Consolatta don't come in pairs in this town. If our Frank raped that girl, Gilbert will roll out every lawyer worth the name. Oh, before I forget, I am his lawyer."

"Now, that's an entirely new facet. Kids!"

"Our best bet right now is damage limitation. Wait a minute: I spoke with her on Tuesday evening. She is in London with my Zina. This means that either she did not tell her father or...." He picked up the principal's letter and read it again. He nodded and smiled.

"Or what, Tony? What? Talk to me, damn it!"

"Or she was not raped. Believe me, if anyone touches that girl, she will tell Gilbert within the hour. Your position as state chief judge will not save Frankie if he raped Gilbert's daughter. This could still be everybody's lucky day."

"Frank swore she surrendered willingly," Nwaeze noted and heaved a huge sigh of sudden relief. "Well, between us, consensual sex is not a crime."

"In this case, I won't go there if I were you."

*

Gilbert saw the State Government Peugeot 505 as it whirred with the air-conditioning unit full blast into his office compound on Zik Avenue. He took no notice until a uniformed police orderly jumped out and opened the backdoor. The big man stepped out leisurely, looking fresh and very important. Gilbert had seen him lately at the Sports Club and at Bishop's dinners. They had not spoken more than salutary phrases to each other since then young and driven state prosecutor called him a thief in an open court.

The intercom interrupted his drifting thoughts.

"Sir, Chief Judge Obi Nwaeze is here to see you," the secretary announced with her eyes popping out of their sockets.

"I will be with him in a minute," Gilbert grinned. The thought of the man's son, anybody indeed, sleeping with his daughter, had shocked and infuriated him. He would have been horrified if it were some loafer, a local lout out to undo everything he had achieved. He had come to terms with the fact that Nnénna was no longer the little girl of yesteryears.

In the waiting room, Nwaeze flipped through glossy foreign magazines and journals. Ordinarily, he would be miles away, but this was very personal.

"Good day, Mr. Iké."

"I am sorry to keep you waiting, Milord."

"Obi Nwaeze will do." He offered his hand leisurely, still sounding arrogant. "Nice outfit you've got here, sir."

"It's a long way from my downtown office, which your rotweillers ransacked while searching for stolen, prewar government cash."

"Please, Mr. Iké."

"Gilbert, please. You were doing your job...." He paused as the secretary rolled in the mobile bar with assorted drinks and refreshments. She deftly pushed the bar into position and left. "Before I talk myself back to court, is this strictly social?"

"I assure you it is very private."

"Brilliant." Gilbert depressed a button, which cut off the secretary and activated a hidden tape recorder. "Help yourself; it's self-service." He took a kolanut of the *cola nitida* variety, split the two-lobed nut with his thumb, and said, "We don't consecrate this type of kola from our Hausa in-laws."

The judge agreed, took the other half, and helped himself to a shot of Remy Martin XO. "I don't know where to begin," Judge Nwaeze began uneasily. "Actually, I would prefer you tell me what you know about Queen's last sendoff."

"What's wrong with a send-off party for students?"

"The Principal alleged that some students played juvenile pranks that allegedly brought the school into public ridicule and disrepute, wherefore and consequent upon the relevant regulations of State Education Board, she is duty bound...."

"Slow down, Judge." Gilbert got a half glass of Florio. "Are we talking about my daughter *dancing* with your son?"

"Frank assured me she consented. Actually, she led him on...." Nwaeze caught himself, paused, and looked at his visibly hurt host. Tony had warned him. It was insensitive and stupid to speak like a tout to a father about his daughter. He was supposed to be the law: Frank was already 18; Nnénna will be 16 in December. He backtracked and said, "You know children of nowadays: fools forever."

"Wait a minute, Judge Nwaeze," Gilbert interrupted his guest's attempt to wriggle out of the gaff of tactlessness. "What Nnénna did or didn't do is nobody's bloody business. She has broken no laws. She is no longer a student at Queen's. Please change the subject. Tell me why you are here."

"I'm sorry, Mr. Iké, but Mrs. Olisa...."

"Excuse me, I am not going to discuss my daughter's private life with you." He walked over to the phone and depressed a red button. "Go on, don't wait for me," he encouraged his visitor and flashed a mechanical smile. "Hello. Who? Oh, Carla, is your mom home? Brilliant, tell her it's Mighty Giles himself." A short pause followed. "Good day, Eva. Mighty Giles here. Oh, she is fine... London. I understand you are taking her to court for bringing...." A long pause ensued at this end of the line. "She's not? No, no, nobody said anything. Is that so? Go get them! Nah, it is no big deal. You want some more? I'll send someone over tonight." Gilbert was grinning and nodding, yeah-ing and nah-ing like a good choirboy.

After what seemed like eternity to the judge, Gilbert spoke again: "Like I said, the wife and Nnénna are in London. I shall join them next month. Yes, I surely do appreciate your concern and cooperation. Don't we all? Don't.... Ha! Ha! Ha! Okay, say me well to the good Doctor. Bye, Ma'am."

Gilbert ignored bemused Nwaeze and pressed a black button. "Tony? Giles here. I have to see you.... What? When? I am sorry to hear that. Why don't you wait until next month; we can travel together? I had booked for Chināsa and myself, but she left with Nnénna. Talking of which, I just spoke with Mrs. Olisa.... You know?" He cast a glance at his worried guest and pointed him to the bar as he continued his lengthy telephone talk. He paused after seven minutes, took some notes, and said, "It's all right then. Seven sharp, tonight."

"Well?" Nwaeze managed to say at last.

"I think you have a private war on your hands. Please keep us out of it, sir. See, if you open many fronts in a war, you will stretch your resources. That was why we lost Biafra. I was there. It was no game. War is raw. People get hurt. People die. It is better to imagine it than to see it. By the way, has Frank told you exactly what happened?"

"You know kids; I nearly killed him."

"That's not how to treat them these days."

"A one-eyed man is indebted to blindness. You do not lose a single palm nut in a spent fireplace: He is my only son."

"True, but you don't smoke out a rat from the yam barn. Nnénna is my only issue; I am not driving around town opening warfronts. We were once like them... well, some of us. Look at my friend, Father Emmanuel Eze, right-hand man of the Bishop: In our college days, mothers held on to their girls whenever we came back from boarding school."

A direct call from the office of the state governor to his red line broke the dialogue. "Giles... Oh, Yerima, how are you? Yes, all is clear. Did you make the cabinet meeting on time? Good. Are you at home now? Okay, let me call you back in a few." Gilbert turned to his guest and said. "Join us this evening at the Sports Club; it's the Governor's monthly visit. I am not sure he will be there though. You and Tony can sort out the loose ends of your war with Madam Principal— Eva... Mrs. Olisa."

"That was His Excellency Colonel Yerima Sambo-Razaq... you will call back?" Nwaeze asked instead.

"Yes, Yerima; he has just been promoted a brigadier and may be leaving for Lagos soon."

"No wonder we waited all last night for him to no avail. He must have traveled to Lagos for briefing."

"No way! He was in my house for a small celebration with some close friends."

"He slept in your house?"

"Yes, my house is his house. With the girls away, we slept late. I feel like Methuselah." Gilbert laughed haughtily. "I bet he is just checking to make sure I am okay."

"You know him that well?" Nwaeze inquired.

"Yerima? He's a brother."

"You don't say!"

"I dare say. Am I missing anything?"

"No, no, it's just something Tony said."

"Take my advice, Judge: don't believe everything Tony says; the man is a damn good lawyer."

"That is not a compliment," Nwaeze observed.

"It is not meant to be, sir," Gilbert sallied. "For the money I pay him, I cannot afford an extra crumb of compliment."

As the Judge walked to his car after the visit, Gilbert chuckled. He chuckled because the Judge must be wondering why Gilbert did not block his recent reappointment by the military administrator. He did not because it was none of his business. His mother made it clear to him that 'killing' comes in many shades. Since every fate is from God, it is foolish to derail the good fortunes of others. He never attempted to influence any political appointments into the current cabinet of Governor Sambo-Razaq. Gilbert was that apolitical.

A loud noise was coming from a passing convey. Young men were chanting the slogan of an organization agitating for the creation of Enugu State out of the current Anambra State.

I lakọ alakọ?	Are you leaving?
Wa!	No!
I sokwe biri?	Are you living?
Ee!	Yes!
Keduzi ka i si enyo anya?	Why then are you peeping?
Onye bi n'ala Enūgwu	Whoever lives in Enugu land
Aghaghị ikete oke nke ya!	Must get his share of the land!

Sang to the tune of *'When the saints go marching in'* — the popular American gospel hymn — the lyrics surprised Gilbert. Whom are they bashing with the carefully constructed lyrics? he wondered. Maybe a political clique is targeting non-native prominent personalities, who are against the creation of new states, or an advocacy group is energizing the base of natives, who are gung-ho about the creation of Enugu State. I hope the coming transition to civil rule will not bring more than its fair share of political insanity, especially after many years of military interregnum. Any mishandling of the transition will simply bring military men marching right back into the power arena, and no one will stop them.

Another Jeep-like jalopy moving in the other direction had a bunch of thugs in it.

What do we want?	Power!
When do we want it?	Now!
If not now?	When?
If not us?	*Onye?*
All we are saying…	Just let us be!
All we are saying…	*Shị a haalụ anyị-e!*

That was new. Apparently, some politicians were already itching to take over the reign of power. Gilbert walked back to the office and asked the secretary to rebook two return tickets to London: one for him — Iké, G. C., another for Tony — Ikpeama, A. C. He planned to stop in Lagos, felicitate with Mrs. Sambo-Razaq and family, and then proceed to London.

17

DANGOYA WAS THE LEAST CONCERN OF TONY Ikpeama as the Lagos-London flight touched down at Heathrow's Terminal 2. He knew not much about prostitutes, but he knew they and politicians share similar goals: They both go where their bread is buttered—as do ordinary human beings, but politicians and prostitutes make a business out of knowing which side is better buttered. Simply put, he hated the guts of politicians. Incidentally, Dangoya had a similar belief; to him, lawyers are learned prostitutes ready to lie for a few pennies.

What Tony did not know as he and Gilbert took the same taxi to North London was that his trip revolved around an offspring of his rich but unprincipled client. Meanwhile, he was visibly worried and impatient to reach his daughter.

As Gilbert alighted, he told Tony to take things easily. "Everything in life is destined. It was very hard for me to let Nnénna be, never interfering with her desires, and yet she hasn't done too badly."

Tony buzzed the doorbell eagerly. Nnénna opened the door. She left as soon as she heard that her father was in town, leaving Zina to her family tête-à-tête. When Tony got the full story from his wife, he sat down and reviewed the options. He decided to take Gilbert's advice: allow Zina to chart the course of her destiny. Tony ruled out abortion. The family is Catholic. Instead, he decreed that they must keep it in the family, no matter what anyone else saw or said.

"You mean we shall lie about this?" the wife asked.

"You leave the lies to me." He turned to the daughter: "Zinachidimma my daughter, can you take the entire seven months here in London or...?"

"I have no choice, do I?"

"Of course you do."

"Dad, I see no other option."

"Okay. You have gone to Boston; from there, you will be going to Dallas, Texas. You will be back by... before the next academic session. Thought about the university yet?"

"It has to be here in England."

Over at the Ikés, things were not quite smooth either. The doctor delivered no miracles. To make sure he was not joggling blanks, he requested for a new set of sperm samples. Gilbert obliged. Chināsa was all too willing to subject the family to any test: sperm-head counts, sperm-tail propulsion, uterine homeliness, vaginal acidity/alkalinity, pulp growth dynamics, fibroid prognosis, spinal tap test, etc.

Gilbert wanted the family to take a break and travel, but Chināsa was not interested. He and Nnénna left for the States. For two weeks, father and daughter toured North America, from Washington, DC to Washington State. It strengthened the bond that her little indiscretion nearly ruptured. He told her about the visit of Frank's father and that the Luxembourg trip earlier in the week was to keep Mrs. Olisa happy.

"You mean Zina's dad knows as well?"

"I don't know what he knows, but I told him I don't want any mentioning of your name... our name. Why?"

"Nothing I can't handle."

"Again? Mommy darling, I am now worried."

"Trust me, this is girlie talk. I might as well tell Zina myself before her father dishes the dirt."

"I doubt we owe Zina or Tony any explanations."

"Daddy, I don't; but girls must be girls."

Zina was getting a lot bigger and feeling a lot better, but her mind kept racing back to that fateful night with Tee Jay. Nnénna noticed and assured Zina that any secret was safe with her. To lighten her thoughts, Zina retold Nnénna the story and added new materials. Obviously, she was slowly recollecting what transpired on that fateful night.

"Hear him: 'You mean you haven't done it before?' Tee Jay said as I tried to restrain his wandering hands. 'Yes and no,' I remember saying. 'You are not a virgin then.' 'It's none of your bloody business…. Stop, Tee Jay,' I protested. 'It's a dirty thing.' 'No way; it's a serious thing,' he assured me. And then this gem: 'A little trial will conceive you'."

"*Conceive?*" Nnénna giggled. "He said that?"

"Conceive or convince, I am not now sure. Whichever, now that I have conceived, I am convinced."

"Anyway, I won't cry rape, but we must make him pay for taking advantage," Nnénna suggested.

"No, let it be the price I pay for causing Consolatta so much pain. We'll keep this between us, right?"

"Sure. Us and your parents," Nnénna added.

"Sure. Now, tell me, what have you been doing? Do not tell me you are still a virgin because I can see through you. This sudden adding of weight and shinning face do not come from eating Yankee hamburgers and English fish and chips. Who is the lucky boy? I hope you didn't sell out to a low life."

She told Zina about the affair with Frank. She expected her to be glad that someone cut Carla down to size. Quite the opposite, Zina hit the roof. She swore and called Nnénna names. "I would not have asked for your help if I had heard about your stupidity. How dare you?"

The reaction came to Nnénna as a complete surprise. "Zina, are you okay?" she asked.

"Why Frank, you bitch? And I thought they called you 'boyfriend snatcher' for nothing."

"Whoa, hold it there: You didn't like Frank, not in that way, or am I missing something?"

"Does it matter? He is befriending Carla—a two-penny pussycat who needs a male body to reassure her that she is alive—but you are supposed to be my friend. Must you?"

"And Consolatta is your enemy... a Miss Nobody? You slept with her boyfriend, Tee Jay, right under her nose, remember?"

"It's different," Zina declared.

"How nice! Educate me, *Miss Ikpeama*." By which Nnénna meant that Zina never backed down in an argument.

"Tee Jay and Consolatta have made up," she said.

Nnénna wanted to add, 'And you are carrying his baby'; instead, she asked, "What makes you think Carla and Frank have not made up? It is not as if I killed him."

"The shock, you blockhead, may *kill* him. How do you expect Carla to recover from the shock? In my case, I was drunk. I have apologized."

"What makes you think I was compos mentis?"

"You wha'?"

"Oh shut up, Zina. You never kissed Frank. You only exchanged juvenile love letters. Tell me, why the sudden rush to Romeo-Juliet rendezvous?"

"You still don't get it, do you?" Zina said and approached Nnénna menacingly.

Nnénna stood her ground with a thinly veiled scorn. "Watch the baby before you commit murder! The sun does not always rise from your bedroom window."

"You piss off, *Ogbanje!* I don't wanna see you again. Ever! You cannot go around snatching people's boyfriends just because you have the money and the license to do whatever you like. Who do you think you are, the Queen of Amazonia? Just naff off, you *Shokolokobangoshay!*"

"Me, Shokoloko?"

Nnénna was surprised and amused at the same time. She had forgotten about the female character from a kindergarten reading and Shokolokobangoshay. It was hard to discern now how she applied to the character. She was sure Zina meant to say *shokoloko*, urban children's term for cow egret, which the Igbo call *ụgbana*. If so, it was apt. The feathers of the cow egret are scarlet white, yet it eats junk meat and feeds on cow ticks, which is why some Igbo folks call it *osoefi* (cow companion). In essence, Zina considered her superficially good looking but character flawed.

Nnénna saw it differently, assuming Zina meant to use the cow-egret metaphor. In her estimation, she was the good-natured person whose plume no stain can contaminate. As the Igbo have it, no amount of dirt discolors the cow egret: *Ụgbana ka e tere unyi n'ahụ, ụgbana achazịa ọcha nke ọ chafọrọ.*

Metaphors and meanings apart, Zina has taken the matter beyond mere friendly misunderstanding, Nnénna thought. She pulled herself back to reality and said, "Thank you, Zina. Thank you very much! Your outburst suits me perfectly. One thing I must tell you is this: your stupid secret is safe with me. I promised, and I shall keep it."

"Go ahead and tell, bloody blackmailing busybody. Go ahead, tell Tee Jay and see if I care."

Nnénna kept looking at Zina as if she were a lost sheep seeking salvation. She tried to smile; instead, she heard herself say to Zina, "Relax."

Zina was on a warpath. To drive home her point, she said, "Do your worst; I don't bloody care!"

"Oh no, you bloody well care. Pick up the phone and call Consolatta; go ahead… give her the *good* news. Go ahead and tell her that you are carrying her boyfriend's baby. You'll make her day, you hypocrite."

"Walk! I don't wanna see you ever, you hear? Go hit the bricks! Get out!"

Nnénna stood transfixed. She sighed and shook her head. She did not know what to feel. Anger? She was not angry. Pity? There was no need for that. Disappointment? Maybe. She needed to tell Zina how she felt, but she was not sure how to phrase it to minimize the impact. She said softly, "You are pathetic. I never thought friends could get this low."

Zina will not back down. "And I say: Piss off!"

Whatever satellite channel Zina had been watching, or whatever movie videos she had sat down to devour, she got value for the time and money invested. The slang Americana definitely came via satellite. Nnénna turned and walked. Now angry and disappointed, she reached for the doorknob.

Nnénna was about to close the door quietly when Zina screamed, "Scram!" She banged the door so hard the hinges groaned.

Zina's mother was coming up the stairs as she stormed down the stairs. "Nnénna, what is it?"

"Please, Ma, ask Miss Zina-knows-everything Ikpeama," she responded and walked out of the house.

"You girls are not going to kill me in a foreign land. What is it that two big girls like you cannot sit down and talk like sisters you are? Here I am pleading that infirmity is not equally distributed and you girls want one with elephantiasis of the scrotum to develop abdominal abscess. Don't I have enough on my plate already?"

Inside the house, Zina was still fuming. "Stupid girl!"

Nnénna stepped out of the perimeter fence. She overheard Mrs. Ikpeama speaking most affectionately to her daughter, "Zinachidimma, what is it, my dear? Are you okay? Come, come, come here. It's okay, my dear."

Nnénna walked the one mile or so home. She wanted to clear her head. The streets of North London were not busy at this time of the day. She walked past people of all races and ethnicities, people she had never noticed.

Nnénna thanked God for the way things turned out. She had gone over to confide in someone she considered a friend. What she had to say could have irreversible consequences on her very being. She had counted on Zina's trust, just as she believed Zina counted on her trust. Instead, Zina called her nasty names, abused her, and threw her of the house.

No matter the issue, I, Nnénna, cannot be this mean to Zina. Carla, I understand; the mulatress has every reason to want to scratch out my eyeballs, though she had it coming. Zina? Why did she freak out like *ekeuke*, the scrawny dogs at Eke Eziuke market? Even *ekeuke* dogs have reasons to bark at everyone and everything–they are considered crazy and are destined to die as sacrificial beasts and discarded. Zina, the daughter of Tony Ikpeama, Senior Advocate of Nigeria (SAN), is a bright star of her generation, supposedly. This is insane.

Nnénna's did not direct her anger at Zina per se but at her stupidity: Friendship is something special to me. I will never compromise again on everything that true friendship means. Friends are supposed to support each other, even die for one another. Friends do not scream when friend's inadequacies become apparent; friends should understand human frailties, the failure of humans to live up to societal set standards. Friends should worry when their friends' actions abuse the trust and the love on which the relationship rests. To everyone, friendship is hope, love, trust, and support. Zina is not an exception; she should not be an exception; and she is accountable for her actions.

Zina, daughter of famous Tony Ikpeama, slashed off yards from the rope of friendship Nnénna had offered, and she hanged herself with it. She showed Nnénna that double standard is real. Zina might not have been what many call 'friend,' but Nnénna believed that they were just that: friends. If they were not friends, why did Zina call for her help, and why did she tell her all about the dalliance with Tee Jay?

Nnénna decided to forgive Zina. In fact, by the time she covered half the way, she knew she had forgiven her. Forgive, yes; forget, no. She bore no grudges. 'Life is too short for hassles of any kind,' she once told her father, but Zina's case was a crooked kettle of corns.

A friend like her father, Nnénna concluded, did not exist out there. She got home and asked him out. Gilbert was all for it and asked Chināsa to come along. She declined. To her, Gilbert and Nnénna were a balanced equation. Like pure oxygen and petrol, they needed no catalyst to burn—just naked flame; they burn other materials that get in the way.

Father and daughter went to a posh wine bar. Nnénna was big for her age and, with her father around, no one asked questions. In any case, she did not drink alcohol, which was easily available at home; she just wanted a quiet outing with her father.

She talked; he listened.

Nnénna poured out everything. Everything.

She was not disappointed: Gilbert is a father and a friend rolled into one and much more. What he heard took some time to sink in, but he stood by her and vowed to be there for her all the way, no matter what it took and no matter what she wanted to do about it. For Nnénna, it was the last hurdle to womanhood, an informal and unplanned rite of passage to maturity. She just arrived in the world of adults, though her father had always treated her as an adult.

"Thank you for the trust," Gilbert offered as they rose to leave the quiet, posh pub by the street corner.

"I should thank you for everything."

Gilbert left London for Lagos after two more trips to mainland Europe, one of which was to pick up some stuff for Mrs. Eva Olisa from her sister in Luxembourg.

18

BACK IN ENUGU, THE ASHES FROM THE ERUPTION of *Mount Finelay* had not settled. By one careless stroke of unstudied wit, she sentenced herself to tough times on any campus. At last, Queen's girls had found something to say about Finlay Nnénna Iké.

The story was an open secret but, inasmuch as Carla wanted to get back at Nnénna, she knew her reputation was also on the line. Fortunately, all the senior girls left after the sendoff. In fact, most students came from their city homes. Only a few girls who were from outside the town stayed the night and left the next day, Sunday.

For Carla, the nightmare continued. She was going for her A-Level at the nearby Federal Government College. Based on her high school grades, the chances of a successful university matriculation were remote. Her father refused to call in any favors for her, which was why she repeated a class.

Despite all the dust her mother the principal raised in the name of upholding the school's honor, Carla still loved Frank. She wanted him back, but his life had taken a bad beating from the *Finelay* affair. His father was still fighting the fire, and his future at the university was now uncertain.

Carla called Frank. They meet at a secret rendezvous the week after his father's frantic shuttle diplomacy. Frank was recovering from his father's physical and mental abuse. Though reprieved that the might of Mighty Giles was not descending on him after all, he still felt bad. Frankly, Frank was making up with Carla only to get her mother off his back. He never loved her as she loved him, but the grass that bows to the storm survives.

In her desperation to drive the fear of infidelity into Frank and to cut down her perceived opponent, Carla recounted and served the shocking stories about Nnénna with liberal spicing for maximum derogatory effect.

"What do you know about *ogbanje*?" Frank asked.

"This one is more than *ogbanje*; she is a mermaid. Do you remember how you just walked out with her from the dance floor?" He did not. "If we hadn't come to your rescue, you could have died. With her father's millions, they could have covered it. You should have seen her after you ran: She glowed like sacred Idemmili python. The girls said she glided like *Mamiwota* the mermaid."

Frank wanted to throw up. He held his nose and opened his mouth. Carla thought she was getting to him. She was. She pressed on with hair-raising lies. As she tried to put her arm around Frank, he recoiled, visibly terrified. Undaunted, Carla pumped in more lies she had made up all week. By the time she remembered to gauge his reaction, it was too late.

"Frankie! Frankie-e! H-E-L-P!"

The doctors at a posh private hospital on Aria Road, just opposite the old European Cemetery, fed Frank intravenously for two weeks. The Nwaeze-Olisa family feud deepened, and the police stayed out of the battle of two Enugu elite families. Legal letters were going back and forth until Tony came back from London.

Tony Ikpeama was not a medical doctor, but he knew that Dick Tiger could not absorb such psychological shocks as Frank had endured. Within days, he cut through the web of half-truths and pure lies and reached the local loudmouth that supplied the devastating tools of destruction to Carla. Armed with a written confession, Frank's problem was half-solved. He needed no modern medication, just tender loving care and proper psychotherapy. Nothing worked. Eyes open, Frank said nothing. Turn off the lights, he screamed.

Things got from bad to worse until a reverend-sister aunt visited. As if possessed, Frank held onto her cross, causing the aunt to request help to maintain her balance. It did not take long thereafter before the nun gained his confidence and pulled him back to the sanity spectrum with daily counseling. As if confessing to a priest, Frank laid it all out and asked for prayers, for forgiveness.

Slowly but steadily, the nun dispelled Carla's lies as the ranting of a jilted lover. "Finlay is an only child. People always make up stories, especially if the child is a girl."

Frank gradually regained his reality, but he did not go back to the university. He traveled with the aunt, who was going on a missionary trip to Rome. It took all of seven years before Frank breezed back into town.

The Nwaeze and Olisa family feud endured. Every noble busybody knew about the case, but such scandals amongst the rich and famous did not appear in government-controlled media. No editor risked his job with a careless gossip about the Sports Club crowd. Truly independent media did not exist in the city; they appeared to support some wealthy politicians and quickly disappeared after elections. National papers were still myopic, focusing only on Lagos life.

The Iké family was away in London and out of the loop of frosty finger-pointing and petty squabbles. Since Nnénna's name was not divorced from the story, Gilbert asked the state military governor to call the two men to order. He did, and the matter died down with deafening silence.

Three months in North London did not cement the bond between Nnénna and her mother. Her resolve to have a son diluted the bond that had blossomed between them. Her mother's attempts to lighten discussions were as disastrous as her endless monologues and inexplicable temper tantrums. Nnénna did not mind; she only missed her father, though he often flew in and out en route to the Far East.

"Mom, why are you looking at me that way?"

"FEN, when did you start wearing padded brassieres?" Chināsa asked pointedly.

"I told you last week I don't wear padded bras, and I am not wearing one now. Do you mind telling me why this sudden interest in my lingerie?"

"Come on, you can trust me. Somebody whose parents we know? Okay, let me guess, you and Zina are experimenting."

"What? Mom, find some other things to joke about."

Nnénna did not know how society saw *supé* during her mother's time, but no one took experimental, high school lesbianism lightly during her time. If it was still rampant, she did not know. At Queen's, everyone knew what *supé* meant, but it was never pop hip, and no one flaunted the youthful act of fleeting lesbianism. Actually, Nnénna was going through hormonal changes, but she and her mother were operating on different frequencies. Therefore, she did not let her mother into the secret she had shared with her father.

Chināsa spent an inordinate amount of time on the phone talking with everyone from Fanny, Father O'Keeffe who had recently moved back to Ireland, and her London gaggle of gossipers to her mother Abigail, stepfather Madaki, and half-brother Zakky. Whenever Nnénna felt like letting her mother into the secret, she would fish out something silly to say. She once tried to tell her mother what happened at the sendoff and the long-term consequences; the next second, she found other people's lives more interesting. Nnénna let her be.

"By the way, FEN, why didn't you tell me Zina's mother came to have a baby?" Nnénna looked at her mother in disbelief. "I saw her at Shepherd's Bush last weekend. She was more than four months gone. How I wish I was like her."

She thought her mother was going goofy and wanted to call her father. "How can Zina's mother be four months pregnant?" Nnénna said almost to herself.

"Come on; give your mommy some credit, girl-child."

"Mom, listen: If it will make you feel any better, we'll go out tomorrow and shop. No, just listen." Chināsa stopped and listened. "Good. We will make you two... three months pregnant like Zina's mom; next month, four, and so on."

"What happens in the end?"

"Premature? We can say it was born dead due to the cold weather. Another miscarriage, stillbirth, something... I mean ... anything can happen. Ambulance men not arriving on time.... We could not sue them because we are not citizens."

"Brilliant!" she exclaimed, mimicking her husband. "Do you know in our place, women carry other people's children to help them conceive?"

Nnénna got up to get a drink. The phone rang. She went for the kitchen receiver and picked it up. She heard her mother already deep in conversation with Zina's mother. She quietly replaced the receiver.

"Mama Zina, you did not notice that I am not far behind you in tummy competition!" Nnénna heard her mother lie. "Oh, yes-o! Thank you. Yes. Mmm, I know. I know. Yes, it is good news all around. Yes. Huh? How is she? Great! Same with FEN here: she is always studying. Good. Yes, we just want to make sure what happened last time does not repeat its evil self. Thank you. Oh, she is here." Chināsa cupped the mouthpiece and hollered: "FEN? Please pick up the phone; it's Zina's mother."

"Hello? Good afternoon, ma'am.... I am okay." Nnénna listened to Zina's mother pleading passionately on behalf of her daughter for rapprochement. Nnénna was adamant. "I am sorry, Mama, but I really don't want to talk about it. No, it is not your problem. I am okay with the situation."

Nnénna looked out to make sure her mother was not within hearing distance and whispered, "I don't think it is safe, since she has to help you with the 'pregnancy'."

Zina's mother did not need any more convincing at this point. She understood that it was for the best and thanked Nnénna for keeping the secret.

Nnénna accepted the kudos, but she declined the offer to speak with Zina on the telephone. "Thanks, but I really must concentrate on my A-Level exams at this point. Maybe when all these happenings settle, we shall reconnect and pick up the pieces. Yes, and I must help my Mom with her shopping, assuming this one stays."

"Your mother said you are both staying back?" Zina's mother asked trying to steer the discussion away from the knotty issue of her phony pregnancy.

"Yes, mainly for observations. Dad refused to bring any of the housemaids. The government says it is slavery here, and I think they are right in majority of the cases. We can manage. Thanks. Sure. Say me well to Zina. Bye."

"She bought it?" Chināsa exclaimed.

"What?"

"That I am pregnant... you know?"

"Are you not?"

"Don't be silly. How am I going to go home with a child in seven... eight months? What are we going to tell your Daddy?"

"We shall tell him that English doctors performed an American abracadabra. You know him; he won't mind."

"Go on then, call him," Chināsa dared her daughter.

Nnénna picked up the phone and dialed their Enugu numbers. Her father was at the Sports Club. He left a message for him to call whenever he came back. "It is very important," she warned the houseboy.

Gilbert called back at about midnight, which was 11:00 p.m. GMT. Knowing the facts, he said he was all for it.

"He bought it!" Chināsa exclaimed. "I don't believe it."

"You better believe it."

19

Nnénna passed her A-Level exams with good grades. The result from previous year's JAMB exam was okay: She got an admission slip from the University of Nigeria, Nsukka, but she wanted to go outside the region, to the other side of River Niger. She concentrated on her A-Level exams in London and applied directly to the University of Lagos's Faculty of Law.

With the closing of Zina's chapter, her time in London was uneventful. By some shock therapy, Nnénna turned her mother around and revealed her situation. Chināsa was in no position to pontificate. Everything fitted as in jigsaw puzzle. They became close, but the trials of searching for a child and finding it under her nose had taken its toll. Chināsa suddenly aged and became as silly as her fake abdominal arrangement. Gilbert spent quality time with them until the end of the year. He hated winter, so he returned to Nigeria for Christmas.

By October the following year, Nnénna came back from her long sojourn in London armed with three A-Levels in English, History, and Government. Zina's parents were on the same flight with a baby boy. Nnénna carried the baby for a while, but she did not ask of Zina, who had gained admission to read law at the University of London.

When Zina had the baby, the Ikpeamas extended a special invitation to the Ikés. Nnénna did not attend; she could not. Gilbert represented the family. Mrs. Ikpeama understood that Chināsa could not come because of her situation, but she expected Nnénna to forgive, if not forget. The birth of a child signals a new beginning and enemies use the event to make up, she preached. Nnénna refused to bite.

At the University of Lagos, Nnénna tried to work out a survival strategy. For starters, she suppressed 'Finlay' in all records outside the registry. As her first name, she rightly chose 'Nnénna,' the name that sounded so sweet only when used by her father—who did not use it much anyway. It was too little too late: three of the girls present on that fateful day at Queen's were studying at the university. They were staying in the same Moremi Hall as Nnénna. Known blabbermouths, they could serve a good gossip to a multitude in minutes.

When a girl from the outskirts of Lagos, who had thought she was too hot to handle, asked to know 'why the Coal City *chikito* thinks we are all idiots,' they told her: 'She has a rich sugar daddy and a fleet of boyfriends.'

"Oh, one more thing about Finlay... Finelay actually: she flaunts it."

Lies, of course, but no one is truly good behind her back. It did not take long for the lies to come alive with short legs. Nnénna was tall, pretty, and chique. The one-year escape to London brought out the *Wonder Woman* in her. It was a milestone; she went straight from hot, high school chick to splendid womanhood. Her classmates still looked girlish at 18. Though younger, she was more mature and exquisitely so. She felt it, and it showed.

"Hello Finelay," a male student said one day by way of sincere-sounding but sarcastic salutation.

"Screw you, Scumbag," Nnénna screamed and regretted it almost immediately. She wanted to apologize, but the big boy with three tribal marks on each cheek had other items on the agenda.

"Wow, did you all hear that?" he exclaimed to attract the attention of passersby. "She is short-fused and foulmouthed too!"

"Ol' boy, chill it," a bigger bloke with a Barry White-like cave-echo voice cautioned.

"Bobo-o-fine, is she your sister? Nonsense!"

"I said, 'Chill it,' or you'll get a free facial surgery."

It became obvious to Nnénna that she was going to live with the ghost of her Queen's prank. She had thought campus was a citadel of academic excellence, a sanity sanctuary in a desert of discord. Instead, some girls were busy slandering her. She might as well turn it into an educational experience. She decided to leave them alone.

A good soul, Nnénna had one very transparent quality: She got along well with all manner of people, as long as they did not try to know her life history or tell her how they lived their lives. She was not interested in anybody's story. She did not have a close relation with any boy, but she enjoyed the company of boys. The first boy she spoke with on campus was different, or maybe someone sent him to check her out. Whatever, the poor fellow needed to know that he was out of his circle; and his deep tribal marks was a turn-off to her.

Nnénna was not short on admirers, but she did not want to get into any serious relationship. She joined no clubs. She avoided the bars. Students who tried to get back at her for no just cause found themselves holding empty baskets. She survived the first term effortlessly. She left campus at the end of the term for Christmas in Enugu.

Her mother brought home a bouncing baby boy. Just as his father named him after his grandfather, Gilbert named the baby 'Nnanna' after his father. Nnénna named him 'Nnamdi' (my father lives). For baptismal name, Chināsa chose Fernando and insisted that they address him so. He is her dream baby: a handsome and healthy medical wonder, or so everyone outside the immediate family believed. Gilbert had a big party. Alcohol flowed and loosened many tongues, tongues of praise and tongues of regret for doubting the trust of Gilbert in God. Chināsa was happy: There is a girl, and there is a boy; my life is complete.

The remaining part of school year was not eventful, but it was still 'Finelay' left, right, and center. She tried to be nice to the student with deep voice, but he was fast becoming her bodyguard. She reckoned that the development might further alienate her. She avoided him. She did not bother to get his name.

The second year, there was no letting up.

"Finelay," one lager lout screamed as she wandered into *Cool Campus Bar* for lack of a better thing to do.

"Yes."

The student was surprised: "Eh ee... mm I just wanna...."

"You just *wanna* be fine-laid?"

Shocked, he shouted, "No!"

"Oh, you are impotent?"

"No!"

Roars of loud laughter enveloped the cafeteria.

"Okay, you don't *wanna* be fine-laid, you don't smoke, and you are drinking Fanta; what else do you do? Have wet dreams every now and then?"

"Answer! Answer!" the girls screamed.

The student slowly recovered in the face of boos and stood up menacingly, "I resent your choice of words."

"And what words do you prefer, since you suddenly find 'fine lay' objectionable... make love?" Nnénna queried.

"Well, yes...."

"Okay, darling lover boy," Nnénna noted and turned to the spectators, "Anyone wants to 'make love'? Please, help this poor bum-boy before he goes completely bonkers."

Everyone laughed and jeered at the chap. Nnénna flashed a sorry smirk, winked, and walked out. All eyes shifted and followed her.

A female student went after her. "Excuse me?"

Nnénna stopped. "Yes?"

"Ekwutosina; 'Tosina for short. Biochemistry."

"Hi, I guess you know mine. Law."

"You see, that's what I want to talk to you about: We don't really know you. We hear you are from Enugu, but that is it, really. George told me he has been trying to talk, but you won't let him."

"Deep Voice?"

"Yes."

"I am not ready for campus love. I have heard it said that the day one looks for a lover is the day lunatics look for wives. I am not looking, and lunatics are all over looking for God knows what."

"You have one less to worry about: The President is taken, and I will make sure it stays that way."

"Oh no, believe me, he didn't make a pass or anything. I don't even know why they call him 'The President.'"

The thought of Carla and Zina sent shivers to her heart. Tosina looked much more mature at about 21. Nnénna did not want to get into a fight for affection with someone in an entirely different league of lovers. In competitive romantic affairs, she was still in Sunday school soccer league.

"I know. He is not that kind at all. When he heard that the posse of provincial area boys and some stupid boys from the bush were abusing you, he just felt a brotherly *love nwantiti*, you know." Tosina flashed a warm smile.

Nnénna knew what 'little love' meant to anyone east of the River Niger: a candid crush. She smiled back.

At UniLag, Nnénna found out soon enough that very little had changed since the 1960s. The ethnic undercurrents were still in existence. It seemed everyone learned little from the 1966 venting of interethnic squabbles. It is useless to build a multiethnic nation on a faulty foundation; the resultant *nation* will collapse on impact with major developments. Such major developments include interethnic crises or, worse, interreligious conflagration.

Nnénna marveled that the streets of Lagos were killing fields only two decades earlier; streets where fellow citizens hounded and hacked her folks to death like stray dogs. She had read that the atrocities were open and organized. She had also read that in all such states of anomy, as the Igbo Pogrom, there are usually telltale signs on the path to perdition. As in all traumatic massacres, from ancient ethnic enmities that date back to the first Homo sapiens, through Euro-driven chattel slavery of Africans to centuries of anti-Semitism that culminated in the massacre of European Jewry in 1940s, there are four basic processes that lead up to such heinous evil:

(a) Remote reason: An excitable resentment by those who consider themselves indigenes—actually earlier immigrants;

(b) Ethno-religious tension between earlier immigrants and more recent immigrants;

(c) Jaundiced Junta: The existence of partisan government that will not protect all the people equally;

(d) Immediate reason: An all-too-obvious pretext to light the pyre must exist, an excuse to launch the genocide.

The details of these developments explain why fellow citizens callously cut down many lives in 1966. Living now in Lagos of the late 1980s, Nnénna understood the dynamics of interethnic undercurrents.

"It could happen again," she told her father the other day. "All our investments in Lagos could go up in flames, again."

"My dear, life is a risky adventure. Anything can happen; however, you do not live your life projecting what could go wrong. You live on the experiences of yesterday and prepare today for a better tomorrow."

"If there is a tomorrow...."

"As sure as there is today, there will be a tomorrow; and our today will shape our tomorrow."

20

TOSINA AND NNÉNNA FOUND EACH OTHER exciting enough to engage in dialogues, but Nnénna was still cautious about girlfriends. She said so. Tosina assured Nnénna that she had seen it all. "Some so-called friends are worse than blood enemies," she stated. "You keep some; you lose some. Don't let one bad experience ruin your fun with friends."

Nnénna was impressed. Nobody had made her feel particularly proud to be Igbo in the land of the Yoruba. She had not thought about her ethnicity. Her father often beat his chest and talked about the War and the inherent drive of the Igbo person to succeed against all odds, but she never felt there was something she could add.

They met again by chance a week later at an off-campus eatery called *Buka Tee*. They walked back to the residence halls together. Unbeknownst to Nnénna, they were staying on the same floor of the same hall. She invited Tosina to her room. Something about her fascinated Nnénna, but she could not put a finger on it.

"Let me ask you a simple and direct question: Why are you interested in me?" The tone was somewhat impolite, but Nnénna needed to remove lingering doubts. She did not know her origin or her surname.

"I am not really sure," she replied, her face lit. "I might get you interested in one of my town guys."

"What's so special about your 'town guys'?"

"Haven't you heard about Anioma boys?"

Nnénna sat up and feigned genuine interest: "No, tell me again—I missed last night's *Nine O'clock* news!"

"They make superb husbands," Tosina replied as she sat on the bed.

"I see. You reckon I have a place in that geo-genetic scheme?" Tosina nodded. "Thank you very much: I won't be a guinea pig, and I don't need a househusband."

"Come on, Nnénna, give us a trial."

"If I want a man to worship me, I'll stay at home: Daddy worships me. If I want a man to lick my feet, I will marry Nicholas; he is our ceremonial chauffeur. Don't get the wrong idea, Nicholas is a hunk; he just didn't break through the academic barrier. I do not need a superb husband. In fact, I am not sure I want a husband at all."

It was a relationship between intellectual equals. They did not stray outside the immediate areas of discussion. No one asked about each other's towns or families. If Tosina had not invoked Anioma regionalism, Nnénna had no way of knowing that she was from the Igbo-speaking area of west River Niger.

The next week, she met 'The President.' George Offiah was a bright student. He ran for the student union presidency in his second year. He was the best of the three candidates, but he lost. George lost to campus ethnic politics. The way many saw it, it would have been easier for a son of Herr Adolf Hitler to become president of Oxford Union in 1945. His mates admitted that George was the best president they never had. This was why they named him 'The President,' not because of the similarity of his names to those of later two presidents of America: In Igbo, *ofia* means 'bush.'

The loss devastated George. He flunked his exams and crashed back to second level. When Tosina came in, he instantly fell for her; she, for him. He became a new person. Together, Tosina and George formed the Oriental Social Club, open to persons from across the southbound River Niger… mostly of Igbo ethnic extraction.

Nnénna struck a wonderful threesome with George and Tosina. His interest in her had been purely platonic, and he told her so. His mighty presence kept annoying flies away. She began to mix on campus. The campus cultists, ruffians, and hotheads had had their rough edges honed by tough examinations that saw off many of so-called 'time killers.' Besides, there was a fertile pool of fresh undergraduates.

The second term of second year, Tosina asked Nnénna to vie for Miss Campus. The pageant was a highlight of annual students' week social activities. Tosina was in Nnénna's room a week before the Saturday of the event.

"Who's Nena I hear of all morning; some top gun's chick? She must have spent a fortune."

"That's you," Tosina declared elatedly. "Well, somebody must have mistakenly left out an 'n'."

"One 'n,' yes; two is deliberate. By the way, who entered my name as Nnénna?"

"Well, I thought up the idea to bury the ghost of Finlay. It is not winning that I am after; the contest is rigged in favor of chicks with strong local connections."

"Tosina, 'Finlay' means nothing to me; it might as well be 'Finelay' or 'Findlay' The name 'Nnénna,' I do not play with; it is no ordinary name. If I want a sexier version, I shall do it myself. Come, why compete if it is not to win? I thought you said that Oriental girls stand out?"

"Yes, but not everybody is comfortable with our social sophistication."

"Tough," Nnénna declared. "Nigeria is much more than this stinking lagoon and its freaking islands. I am contesting, and I am in it to win."

On Sunday, Nnénna attended Beach Party, organized by Reggae Club in association with 'Club C@$#,' so-called because it was sponsored by mushroom millionaires with dubious sources of wealth.

Nnénna was dressed in a floral dress with a yellow chic hat to match. Her glasses were like mirrors from horror movies: When you look at them, you hate what you see. On Nnénna, they looked like someone was shooting an episode of a soap opera in Lagos. She walked with a tasteful touch of Dominique Devereaux defiance in *Dynasty* and provocative poise of Pamela Erwin in *Dallas*.

Nnénna walked seductively amidst whistles and catcalls. There was a huge applause when the master of ceremony introduced her as one of Miss Campus contestants. Girls were particularly impressed. They admired her courage and her style. Suddenly, as if cued in by an invisible director, the Oriental Club chicks entered the scene chanting their resolve to support Nnénna: "*Nnénna, Nnénna, Nnénna ka anyị ga-eso.... Ma ọ na-eje eje, ma ọ na-abịa abịa, Nnénna ka anyị ga-eso!*"

Every student sang along. Nnénna was impressed. She regretted going into her shell for so long, albeit instinctive. As a fowl new to a place does, she stood on one leg to test the ground. 'The goal of every animal is self-preservation,' her father had told her. She believed it. She had done it her way. She was going to start living.

One of the beautiful finalists at the well-attended evening show was an Idoma girl called Ene Oyibo. A black beauty, she hailed from a Benue State community northeast of the university town of Nsukka. She was a natural, and she spoke well. Many students had never seen her; she was a beautiful bookworm glowing in her own world.

It was a shame to lose Miss Oyibo, but she could not make up for 25 points, since she flatly refused to parade in a bikini. So, after the elimination rounds, three contestants remained: Fatima Adiza Yakubu, Bimbo Braimoh, and Nnénna Iké. The audience applauded, but some smart sod spotted something.

"QUO-TA?" he heckled.

"SYS-TEM!" responded others as if on cue.

Soon the hall was abuzz with the call and its response: Quota?! System!

Many chanted for the fun of it, but a vocal minority group leader did not find the apparent tripod result funny: "Why must everything revolve around Hausa, Igbo, and Yoruba?" Somebody had gone out and coined a new lingua franca called 'WAZOBIA,' from the words for 'come' in the three languages: *wa* (Yoruba), *zo* (Hausa) and *bịa* (Igbo). It did not stop there: the new lingo derived words mainly from the big three. For example, the term for 'please, give me money' is *biko* (Igbo for 'please'), *fun mi* (Yoruba for 'give me') *kudi* (Hausa for 'money'). The scheme died naturally like all artificial newspeaks.

This day, it was fun, not because the university was a melting pot but because Adiza turned out to be an Igbo girl. She had retained the names she used in high school to secure free education in predominantly Muslim north. In addition, Bimbo was not a true representative of one of the big three because her father was of Edo ethnic extraction. Nnénna was understandable because George made it known during the campaign. According to him, "There are certain things in this country that will not look right if an Igbo girl is not in it. Beauty is one; brain, the other." Questioned about brawn, George said that was where Igbo men stepped in.

Adiza knew her geopolitics, but she had no hobbies. She played no instruments, could not recite a poem, could not sing, and she found it hard to coordinate her smiles. She wanted to marry, settle down, and produce a football team. It was down to two: Bimbo and Nnénna.

Natasha Abimbola Braimoh had correct curves, correct connections, and popular pageant complexion. She cat-walked with a professional posture, a walk many people found a bit strange. She threw her legs about so much her big boobs jiggled with little restraint.

Interview time, Bimbo showed she had sexy smiles to match her nice pair of legs. "I was born in Odessa, Georgia. My mom is from Soviet Union. I went to an exclusive private school in Barking, Essex, England in the United Kingdom of Great Britain and Northern Ireland."

Bimbo was not a bimbo; she could read the audience. She knew when to stop throwing in names from outside the shores. Her major problem was that she lived in a social circle different from that of her audience. She spoke endlessly when answering a simple question, smiling unnecessarily and flirting with the compeer. Then the murmuring of students turned into loud protestations. The compeer stepped in, not to stop her but to ask if she spoke "very fluent Soviet Union."

"A little," she replied with a sissy voice. "When I was little, I spoke it so well."

"Hear, hear: She speaks Soviet Union," someone yelled, but no one else noted the slaughter of semantics.

A cosmetics company sponsored Bimbo for the contest. Commercial beauty apart, she knew next to nothing about anything outside Lagos. Asked the capital of Bornu State, her bemused look showed she did not care if it was Bornu or Bonzo. "Has Sokoto a Sultan or an Emir?" Bimbo stood there blank. The compeer made up a quiz to get her some points. He asked her the titles of traditional rulers of Oyo and Ife; she came up with 'Oba.' It was accepted. Strictly speaking, she was wrong, but Alaafin of Oyo and Ooni of Ife are *oba* (traditional rulers) in Yorubaland.

Nnénna had a hitch too. Tosina thought she had blown it. She knew her state capitals and names of obscure military governors; some of them had attended her father's parties with the amiable army officer she called 'Uncle Yerima.' The last question was whether Kaduna had an emir or a sultan.

"Neither sultan nor emir; a Gwari chief, probably."

Everybody laughed.

"Booboo!" some students shouted.

The compeer apologized and made up another question. Many Nigerian students knew that Britain exiled King Jaja to Barbados; asking for the date of his arrival was expecting too much. March 1, 1891 never etched on national conscience, but Nnénna knew the date. She did not only ace History of West Africa in West African School Certificate (WASC) exam, she had just submitted an essay on the colonial 1891 trial of King Jaja in Accra, Ghana—then Gold Coast.

"And the winner is Miss Nenaaaaa Iyke!"

A thunderous applause acknowledged the close but easy-to-call decision. Bimbo Braimoh showed her disappointment by walking off the stage without offering Nnénna a hug, her face red with rage.

Nnénna's coronation opened a floodgate of admirers. George took over, handled press releases, set up commercial ads, and charged appearance fees. Nnénna wanted no part of his social schemes. George was undaunted. Her room became the place to be. Nnénna moved out to Tosina's room. They followed her.

To keep things under control, she agreed to meet the growing army of admirers at off-campus events. George moved in and worked wonders. Tosina did not bargain for this outcome. She refused to attend any of the off-campus parties. She knew the sort of people using George as a front. She loved George and could do nothing to rain on his bliss, so she warned Nnénna to back off before she got hurt.

"Don't worry about me," Nnénna assured Tosina. "I am not enjoying all the attention, but I don't want to look back years from now and say, 'Had I known'."

"I know, but this thing is going to his head."

"Wait a minute: are you worried about losing George, or are you worried about my safety?"

"Your safety, of course; he is a big boy."

There were parties for Nnénna from Friday through Saturday to Sunday. If she passed a class test, there was a party. If she was flying to Enugu for a weekend, there was a sendoff. On coming back on Sunday, there was a welcome party. Real parties were happening every weekend at Federal Palace Hotel, Victoria Island, Durbar Hotel, a millionaire's cozy hideout, etc. Taiwan tycoons—the new rich—were around to pick up the tabs.

Hangers-on and macho layabouts were many. No-future-ambition chicks were a dozen a dime. Together they formed 'O-O Group,' time-killers on campus. George spoilt party sponsors with choice of girls, but he had screening criteria so as not to devalue events. To give the parties a respectable façade, he called many parties 'charity events.' The monies raised went straight into his pocket.

The more Nnénna saw of the debauchery of mushroom millionaires, the more she recoiled from getting involved with any man. A week before last lecture week, she confronted Tosina and demanded to know what was wrong with her, why she was avoiding all social events since she became Miss Campus.

Tosina told her. She was married at 17, fresh out of high school, to one of those new millionaires. He was not involved in shady deals, but success attracted all sorts of snakes. He died mysteriously. The day after his burial, it was as if she did not exist. Nobody asked how she was doing, where she was going, or how she was going to cope without a husband. Instead, relatives were busy putting together a consortium to house their individual interests. She stayed for four more days and drove west across the River Niger to Asaba.

She came to University of Lagos to get out of their way and, inadvertently, she piloted her way back into the midst of mad moneyed men.

21

Nnénna was so moved by the story she forced herself to open up to Tosina. She confided in her that the car that took her to parties belonged to the Lagos office of her father's business. The driver, whom they nicknamed 'Pocket Powerhouse' because of his short and stocky frame, was a part of the company's human resources. "Colonel Zakky Madaki, the army officer who visits me, is my uncle. The young companion is his ADC … aide-de-camp, Lieutenant Dagogo Fynecountry."

In sympathy with Tosina's trial and tribulation, Nnénna backed off from parties. Besides, exams were approaching. Sensing Nnénna's disinterest, George co-opted Bimbo, the runner-up, and found a very malleable tool for his schemes. In effect, George became her pimp. He dropped off academic radar for the term, and he began to part ways gradually with Tosina.

After their exams, Nnénna felt confident enough to take Tosina home to their Victory Island mansion. Gilbert was on his way out of the country, and he wanted to see Nnénna. Since she did not want her parents coming to the campus, Gilbert sent Pocket Powerhouse to get her.

Tosina watched with wide-open eyes as father and daughter embraced and hugged like a couple on honeymoon. Gilbert was happy to see Nnénna with a friend, especially after the apparently inexplicable bust-up with Zina. He noticed Tosina's discomfiture and coughed.

"Oh, Daddy, meet Ekwutosina; Tosina, my father."

"I am pleased to meet you, sir."

"You are welcome, Ekwutosi," he said and offered his hand. "Are you from Onitsha on the Niger?"

"No," she said, "I am from this side of the River."

"Ah, I had a good girlfriend from Asaba during the war. That was before you girls were born."

Tosina smiled. She was a child of the war, and she has a twin brother named Osondu, meaning 'the flight for life,' to prove it.

Nnénna knew her father could not resist digging into the girl's background. The 'good girlfriend from Asaba' was just a ploy to ferret information without being impudent. She could never understand why people bother with ancestry.

Stereotype or not, people's origins, in Gilbert's books, is a fair pointer to what they might be. Nnénna did not subscribe to the curious hypothesis. "Tosina, this way."

"Hey, aren't you going to ask what Mom prepared?"

"Mom is here?" Nnénna fired back. "With Nnamdi?"

"Slow down; it's 'Fernando,' remember! No, he's at home; we don't want to shuffle him in and out of planes yet."

"She is shopping, no doubt."

"No. Actually, she went to see Zakky at Federal Palace Hotel. He's been posted to Jaji." Nnénna knew. "She will be flying back later today. So, if you have any plans, I am game." He winked.

Nnénna smiled and pulled Tosina away.

"Mom?" Tosina heard herself say as they entered her upstairs room. "Is it your mom... as in biological mother?"

"Yes." Sensing some disbelieve, she added, "You know, like the wife of my father... that sort of thing."

"Oh," she said, perplexed.

"Oh? You thought I walked out of the sea. Tosina, I am their only issue. Not adopted, no step-nothing."

"Who then is Fernando Nnamdi?"

"Oh, sorry, I meant the only daughter. He is only three… a late arrival, the almighty male."

"Wait, you mean the man we met back there is your father, as in F-A-T-H-E-R?"

"What is this? Give it to me straight; I can handle it."

"Okay," Tosina said after a brief hesitation. "The story is that he's your *daddy* quite alright, but...."

"But he is my *sugar* daddy, right? Well, he is not; you can go back and tell them."

"You said I should level with you."

"I'm sorry, but you have got to trust me if we are going to be good friends."

"A friend is a friend; we should not categorize."

"Good."

"Please, if he's available, I will not mind-o!"

"Tough luck, he's spoken for… by my Mom, remember?"

Tosina wondered why her friend wanted to live on campus with what her father had on Victoria Island. Nnénna agreed to move out of the dorm, if she came along and shared the outhouse apartment called 'Boys Quarters.'

They were cleaning the furnished flat when Chināsa came to announce that she was leaving for the airport. They walked across the lawn to bid her safe journey.

"FEN, I don't understand why you want to stay out there." Chināsa knew the matter was not debatable, but she still wanted to air her opinion. Nnénna held the backdoor and said nothing. "Stubborn as ever," Chināsa added as she hugged her.

"Bye Mom, and give Fernando my love."

"I will. You girls, watch out for wolves!"

"Thank you, Ma'am, for everything," Tosina said.

Gilbert came back four hours later. The girls were already dressed for bed; they were watching a movie video in the main house.

"Ladies, the coast is clear! Let's get out and watch the waves rule the ocean." He wore a mischievous smile like a youngster whose parents went on vacation and left him with a kid sister and a girlfriend.

"Not Lagos Victoria Island Club?"

"It's LAVIC Special; a jazz band is playing tonight."

"No, Daddy; if you don't mind...."

"I do. You don't leave campus to imprison yourself here." He went upstairs whistling, but he knew she was not coming.

Tosina did not ask if she was invited or not. "Don't stop because of me, Nnénna. I will not abandon this movie for some local Ella Fitzgerald."

"No, I don't like LAVIC crowd: moneybags and top state VIPs showing off their latest girlfriends and salivating over single ladies. You want to go?"

Tosina sat up. "Are you sure?"

"Last Friday of the month is boys' night out."

"They don't admit women?"

"No wives; unaccompanied girls are welcome."

"Do their wives know?" she asked needlessly. "Typical of Nigerian women, they all sit back and take it."

"No, they don't all sit back." Nnénna explained: "One woman tried to break the taboo. Her husband phoned the Club and got clearance. Before they arrived, all the girls had moved to another hall. The woman saw for herself why it is 'boys' night' out. Everybody was buying her whatever she wanted, encouraging her to drink, telling her to relax, and being nicely nasty... basically. She felt so uncomfortable she begged to go home. They begged her to stay and keep them company... that they could do with a woman in their midst, but she had seen enough. They ran her home in a Supreme Court judge's official, chauffeur-driven car complete with seven police motorcycle outriders blaring sirens."

"Men!"

"Tosina, you can't fight centuries of...." The phone rang. She picked up the receiver. "Hello? Mom! How is Fernando doing? Good. No! Yes, he is getting ready for the LAVIC do. Yes, as usual. No, Tosina and I are staying in. Is she in town? Oh, she is flying into Lagos just for tonight? No, I do not particularly want to see her. Okay. I will get him. Daddy! Mom is on the phone." Nnénna dropped after Gilbert had picked up his extension.

"Did she get home all right?" Tosina asked.

"I guess so. It was her I spoke to, for sure!"

"You know what I mean, Nnénna: The coast is now clear. Now, tell me, so we are really not going?"

"Yes, we are *really* not going anywhere."

The friendship between Nnénna and Tosina grew. They exchanged little secrets as trust deepened. Few people knew that Tosina had twin babies. She was two months pregnant when her husband died mysteriously. She reverted to her maiden name. Her father was of Efik ethnic extraction, but the man existed only in name. She had never seen him, and she never asked her mother what happened. The story she heard growing up was that he was killed during the war. She grew up in Benin City and identified with her maternal Asaba ancestry, the only lineage she knew.

Tosina lived for her twins. She planned to take the boy back to his father's folk as soon as he came of age. Until then she had him wrapped up like a piece of precious painting by Michelangelo.

George felt marginalized, but he was too engrossed with moneymaking ventures to bother. He visited occasionally; at other times, they lunched at Campus Canteen.

One Saturday morning, Nnénna left early as usual to jog along Bar Beach before loafers, layabouts, and the religiously unbalanced took over the white sands of Atlantic coast off the Gulf of Guinea.

Tosina was not into jogging. She normally made breakfast before Nnénna got back. They then tidied up together, dressed up, and drove into the school compound. Nnénna decided to shop on her way back and save them leaving the campus early to shop for food.

Going into a local market was one thing; getting around was another. Haggling was a national religion. No local bought anything without haggling, even if he or she could afford the commodity at posted or requested price. Nnénna indulged for fun; she enjoyed the hospitality of haggling.

She took a taxi back. They used a big freezer in the kitchen of the main house because a dedicated generator switched on automatically on power failing, which was often. On hearing running water, she freed her shopping bags.

"Giles love, I'm in the bath."

Giles love? It was a familiar female voice. Nnénna's head went into a slight spin. She held her breath. She had never thought her father was beyond having an affair, but she had never had a reason to suspect him. Simply put, she never thought about it. It is not possible... not here, she reasoned.

Nnénna walked out of the house. She went straight to her room in the outer apartment. She lay there tired, not knowing why she was upset. She felt a certain bond with her mother, something she had never felt, not even when she was a child.

She got up and got ready to do battle for her mother. She felt like she had personally betrayed her by not confronting the feisty female interloper. Suddenly, something struck her: She was not protecting her mother's turf; she simply could not accept another woman in her father's life. Chināsa was enough—she is her mother; another woman is an unwanted entity. Nnénna's thinking begged the question: How will her father handle the introduction of another man in her life, in the perfect equation that her mother Chināsa was but a spectator ion or, at best, a spent catalyst?

Nnénna thought of how her father must have felt when she told him about Frank. She decided to lick the proverbial hot soup slowly, but some seriously troubling thoughts lingered in her mind: "Who is the lady? It is definitely not Tosina. I would kill her," she mouthed audibly and smiled.

"Tosina, Tosina," she said, knocking concurrently on her bedroom door. She opened the door; Tosina was not there. She went into the kitchen. Her breakfast was on the table, neatly laid out. Beside the coffee cup was a letter. She smiled, poured herself a cup from the Thermos flask, added milk, and took the tray to the common lounge, the sitting room.

She read the letter:

> My darling Nné,
>
> I have to leave for Benin City. My mom called as soon as you left. Something about the twins... nothing major. I decided to leave immediately to get back early enough tomorrow. I'll miss you.
>
> Enjoy your meal and take care.
>
> Love, Tosina
>
> Ps: Nné-o, there is a lady, I mean L-A-D-Y, that Pocket Powerhouse dropped off as I was leaving. I had to come back and register my impression. I tell you, my dear, God molded her on Eke—the morning of creation.
>
> Pss: Please, please get the gist and keep it warm. I cannot wait to hear all about this angel made flesh.

Nnénna smiled and then laughed. She felt stupid. She knew who it was; the only person it could be: Fanny. Nnénna never liked her. When she went to Las Vegas with her father, Fanny surfaced there. It was the very first time she noticed Fanny's curious closeness to her father, which she resented instantly. Thereafter, she noted on more than four occasions that Fanny's feature perfume hung around her father's office. Surprisingly, her mother Chināsa still regarded Fanny as her best friend, and it troubled her.

Nnénna woke up reluctantly to light persistent pounding on the netted storm door. In her sleepy brain, she reckoned that a criminal does not have the decency and the time for niceties, and the gateman will not let in a stranger. She got up, a light *abada* wrapped around her chest-full of treasures.

"Good evening, Dagogo. What are you doing here?"
"Hi, Nnénna, am I not going to get a hug?"
"No, and you are not coming in either!"
"Is it that bad… the distrust for military men?"
"Yes-o! It is too risqué to hug one in this state of undress."
"Okay, I will wait in the car while you freshen up…."
"And then?" Nnénna asked and skewed her eyes.
"I will take you out for an evening of entertainment."
"Officer, does this place look like an army whorehouse?"
"What if your father asked me to check you out?"
"I would call you a bloody liar."
"Okay, what if I tell you I am ordered by my superior to bring you to Ikoyi because Grandpa Madaki is in town?"
"Come in, you town clown."

Dagogo drove Nnénna across Lagos to Zakky's house. Madaki was on his way to London. Grandma Abigail was there too, but she was not traveling with him. She was staying with Zakky's family while he settled down up north.

At about ten o'clock, Dagogo drove Madaki to the airport in the company of Nnénna and dropped him off. Thereafter, they drove to *Deep Dunk*, a nightclub in the same Ikeja vicinity, and partied until the wee hours of the morning. Dagogo was as dunked in booze as fish is in water. Nnénna took the keys. He did not resist; he could not. Once they hit highway and the morning Atlantic breeze hit him, he coiled up and slept like a premature big baby.

He was still dozing on the sitting room sofa when Tosina returned, twenty-four hours after Dagogo first knocked on the netted storm door. Nnénna was not at home.

22

NNÉNNA GRADUATED WITH HONORS. SHE COULD not wait to get Lagos out of her system. Eziuke was bestowing a traditional title on her father. She invited Tosina, George, and members of Oriental Social Club. Zakky and Dagogo needed no special invitation. That summer was hectic. The military was still in power and promising economic miracles. Nnénna was not interested in politics; political power did not feature in her life's agenda.

October, Nnénna went back to Lagos to complete her legal studies at then only campus of Law School. She had some time on her hands, so she decided to give in to Dagogo's advances. Something was not quite right. They were too comfortable with each other, and yet they could not bring themselves to go beyond hugs. Either he was fearful of what Zakky might do to him, or she was still not ready for serious relationship, especially since he was traveling to the United States of America for further studies. She confided in Tosina, who still stayed at the apartment while she waited for her employer to provide a decent accommodation in Lagos.

Zakky noticed the closeness of Dagogo and Nnénna. He informed Chināsa, who promptly summoned Nnénna to Enugu. She took an early morning flight. She had planned to stay away for a week and spend some time with her father, but she could not keep what she heard to herself. On Sunday evening, she flew back to Lagos. There was a lot of noise coming from the main house. Thinking it must be Fanny and her lately endless parties, she went to the outer apartment. Tosina was not there.

Nnénna watched some television shows and slept off on the couch. When she woke up at about 5 AM, the party was over. She walked over to the house. The living room was a mess. In her bedroom, she saw Tosina and Dagogo in a baby-sleeping bearing, burnt out and both butt naked.

Obviously, Tosina chose the weekend of her travel to organize a sendoff for Dagogo in a house she was not supposed to enter. She had never hidden her love and lust for Dagogo, but Nnénna thought she was just joking. Nnénna walked away, dressed up, and checked into a hotel. Midday, she called the Lagos office of Giles International and arranged for a total cleanup. As soon as a cleaning crew arrived, Tosina and Dagogo counted their teeth with their tongues.

The following week, Nnénna was at Murtala Muhammed International to bid Dagogo a safe trip. She told him what her mother had said: they were cousins; the colonial civil servant who fathered her mother was his paternal grandfather. They were both relieved. Dagogo was not surprised; Zakky had hinted him of the possibility. Nnénna did not speak with Tosina. Soon after check-in formalities, she left with Zakky. Tosina stayed with Dagogo in the departure lounge.

The following months, she buried herself in studies. After law school, administrators at National Youth Service Corps (NYSC) sent her to the northern state of Kaduna. Dagogo wrote her several letters, but she did not respond. George moved to Abuja. He was making brisk business in public relations and soon forgot about Tosina, who also moved on with her life; she contacted neither Nnénna nor George.

There was not much to miss in Lagos. It was a vibrant city but not a place for a homely girl from Enugu. In Kaduna, she underwent military-style orientation. Her Campus Queen fame followed her. She did not exploit it. She was determined to make the best of one month of regimented life. She learned to speak passable Hausa.

Zakky lived about 20 miles away in Jaji, halfway between Kaduna and Zaria. He visited often and took Nnénna and her hangers-on out to eat. He had selfish agenda; Nnénna knew. She was not angry. Many military men were at it. One evening a low-flying plane from nearby defense academy disrupted a scheduled evening drill. She knew why: A top officer could not wait an extra hour to pick up his girlfriend. She took in a good dose of military discipline, meted out by army non-commissioned officers as if they resented perceived privileges of academic successes.

After the orientation, NYSC deployed her to the state ministry of justice. She lived with Zakky in Jaji and shuttled to work with an army bus that went up to Kaduna to pick up expatriate lecturers of Command and Staff College (CSC), who were housed somewhere in the city. She never met them; she dropped off before they got on board, and she boarded the bus on its way back from dropping them off. On some days when she worked late, Zakky picked her up.

The senior state prosecutor did not waste time before making a move. She told him bluntly that Idi Amin Dada had a better chance of becoming King Idi of the United Kingdom. He laughed disdainfully at first. He tried repeatedly, but Nnénna firmly rebuffed him. When he tried to force a physical contact, she gave him a knee-to-groin kick that kept him out of office for a week.

Nnénna was very determined to do her part for the legal system, but her big boss berated her beyond her wildest dreams. The country did not address sexual harassment at workplace; it just did not exist: If a man *chases* you, you can always say no—if the proposal is not right. Nnénna did not want to start any crusade. She did not understand feminism, *womanism*, girl-child, and women-lib issues. She knew that a casual whisper to Zakky was all she needed to make her boss wish he never met a girl called Nnénna Iké.

Her boss was frustrated. Verbal attacks and unnecessary officious attitudes did not work. Then he saw Zakky picking her up one day, and he understood 'why she is bragging.'

Three months on the job, he assigned Nnénna to a very difficult and sensitive case. The police had milked the accused of so much money, and the state knew it. Giving the case to a greenhorn was like throwing a novice gladiator into a den of deliberately starved lions.

Nnénna borrowed Zakky's car for the week and took a mountain of legal paperwork home on Friday. On Monday morning, she called in the police officer in-charge of the case and threatened to send him to jail unless he leveled with her off record. He complied.

The case of advanced-fee fraud came up in Court No. 1 the following Monday. She asked the court to quash her first case before it started. Her boss was furious. He vowed fire and hailstone. Nnénna was resolute. Arguing convincingly and calmly, she submitted: "Any person in England who pays £500,000.00, allegedly, to a faceless fellow in Nigeria with eyes on a £50-million contract has no good intentions.

"Milord," she concluded, "This is a classic case of so-called '419,' but those who seek justice must come with clean hands. The accuser should indeed be the first accused."

Nnénna cleared her desk and drove to NYSC secretariat. A formal letter stated her reasons for seeking redeployment. The office reassigned her to GIZAM Arewa Produce, Ltd., a company that exports groundnuts and sundry produce.

Nnénna was happy at GIZAM. They gave her a car. She lived with Zakky, but his drinking and womanizing now bothered her. One Friday night, he came back with two girls. He asked one to share the guestroom with her. Nnénna left the bed for the trollop and slept on a couch in the large lounge. Early Saturday morning, she packed her things and checked into a hotel.

On Monday morning, she told her boss at GIZAM that she needed the accommodation he had offered her at the company's guesthouse.

That evening, Zakky showed up at the door. "Young lady, you have given me white hairs these past days!" he yelled. "If you want to live here, we shall live here, together. Look at me when I talk to you, damn it! I am sorry about the other night; it won't happen again." He held her half-affectionately.

"Tell that to your wife. Let go," she demanded.

A week later, she was rereading the recommendations in a report she had prepared. A knock on the door between her office and that of her boss startled her. She looked up.

"Father! What are you doing here?"

"I should be asking that question. Adamu," he said to her boss, "what is this girl doing here?"

Adamu was speechless. It had occurred to him when the girl gave him her curriculum vitae that she could be a relation of the managing director, but "Iké" is widespread... as are many simple Nigerian surnames.

"*Wallahi tallahi*, I didn't know she is your daughter, sir," Adamu swore.

"What are you two talking about?" Nnénna was visibly surprised.

"It's all right, Adamu; please leave us for now." He did. "Hello Mommy. How did you do it? I thought you wanted to stay out of the nest for NYSC year."

"Could you please stop speaking in parables?"

"Nnénna, my love, 'G' is Gilbert—your Daddy."

"'I' for Iké and 'ZAM' is Zakky Abbas Madaki!"

"Good guess. Don't worry; I won't interfere."

"Like hell you won't. No wonder Zakky is...."

"Nnénna, my love, have I ever interfered?"

She shook her head and then said, "I don't recall."

"Brilliant. If I could let you be when you were at Queen's and at UniLag, why would I suddenly want to interfere?"

"So who told you I work here?"

"No one said a thing to me. If I had known it was you, I would have gone back to my hotel and flown out. Adamu insisted on showing off a legal luminary he had recruited. He had gone ahead and prepared a contract agreement for your employment as our company's legal adviser. He was so thrilled I decided to see this female 'Lawyer Ikpeama' before I sign the papers. Now, do I get a hug or what."

She embraced him, but not so warmly.

"Are you all right, Mommy?"

"I am all right, Father."

"Father! No more 'Daddy'?"

"There is Daddy and there is daddy."

"But I am your father."

"Which is why I called you 'Father,' not 'Daddy'."

"Why?"

"Many daddies are now sugary."

"Look, I don't know what your generation is up to these days. Come on, let's go have lunch and talk."

"I have to give my boss a report before noon."

"And if your boss's boss says no?"

"I will say he is interfering!"

They laughed heartily.

The company driver took them to Ahmadu Bello Way, to Mama Calabar Restaurant. The afternoon special dish was *edikaingkong*, a vegetable-and-meat potpourri served with pounded yam. Periwinkle was a part of the army of edible ocean-dwelling creatures in the popular Efik-Ibibio dish. Alas, in Eziuke, any creature in a hard shell and does not bleed is taboo.

They moved over to Durbar Hotel and had white rice and beef stew.

23

NNÉNNA DROVE GILBERT TO THE AIRPORT.
"You sure all is well between you and Zakky?" Gilbert asked on the way.

"You know Zakky, 'the cold colonel from Cucumberland.' He has not seen his family in three months. I do not care about his female corpers, but he is overdoing it. If nobody tells him, I shall."

Gilbert pleaded with Nnénna to take it easy with her maternal uncle, especially in public. "It's not your fight. Man-woman bond is not skin-deep. Do not try to understand it. Each couple has its peculiarities. Men who decide to settle down surrender to the magic of matrimony. The rest resorts to rebellion. Question: If men know the headache involved, why marry and remarry? Why stay married? I will tell you why men must marry: mommy dearest has programmed and conditioned them to succumb to the wonders of womanhood. A chauvinistic elder once told me: Whomever a woman does not kill lives long. So men must surrender or die."

Nnénna did not quite understand what her father was saying with that piece of philosophical professing, but she promised to back off and added lightheartedly, "I must-o, especially now that I know those that own GIZAM."

"Don't let that be a factor; you have a bigger share."

"For real? From you and Grandpa, I bet."

"Zakky too; it's all in black and white. By the way, when are you going to give Tosina and Dagogo another chance?"

"I don't want to talk about them."

"Just remember that Dagogo is family."

"Daddy!"

Nnénna had read her basic rules of friendship to Tosina. If she could not trust her to keep her legs closed in the company of her friends and family members, she was never a friend. She tried to compare Tosina's treachery with Zina's zeal, but she switched her mind to other things as her father steered her to the first-class restaurant for brunch.

While they ate, Nnénna told her father about her findings, after extracting a promise not to use them against Adamu.

"He is a nice man. It is not his fault; he did not have to put you onto the trail of any deals. He had told me about it but, because it didn't influence our company's account directly or negatively, I told him not to worry," Gilbert chuckled. "Apparently, he kept snooping and got nowhere, until my Nnénna came. This is why we need a good corporate lawyer."

Nnénna thought about it. The obvious fraud she had uncovered at GIZAM did not benefit the company. Her father was probably doing a friend a favor, or he was paying an old debt. In a normal society, someone would be behind bars. Nigeria is not a normal society; it is a society where strange things happen normally, a state where strange situations are standard.

Since she was now a part of the setup, she decided to level with her father. "GIZAM must cut that end loose ASAP."

"Why?" Gilbert wondered.

"Such deals cannot hold up to sustained scrutiny. The money involved is just too much. If we are supplying military hardware, no one will mind. No military establishment in the world spends that much money on food."

"Not even in war?"

"Dad, even if you are feeding the armies of the entire continent of Africa, the money involved is still suspicious. Here we are talking about the contingent in Liberia. No, it is not worth it. Tell Uncle Yerima to backpedal and to tell his superiors to find a more credible money-laundering method."

In bed at GIZAM Guesthouse, Nnénna allowed a deep thought of her split with Tosina for the first time in many moons. She had been in denial, and she knew it. Her father had just punctured her bloated bubble. It suddenly dawned on her that she had been fighting Zakky and his flock of floosies for mostly the wrong reasons.

Dagogo spent nearly two years abroad and earned a master's degree in political science. Tosina had joined him after six months. They came back at the tail end of Nnénna's national service. The military posted him, as they say in their parlance, to Nigerian Defence Academy (NDA), Kaduna. Tosina travelled to Benin City to stay with her mother until he secured a befitting accommodation. Two days later, Dagogo showed up at Nnénna's office and invited her to lunch.

Nnénna took the day off. Half an hour into the drive, on the road to Kano, she said, "We have passed Jaji."

"I know," Dagogo said, smiling.

Nnénna relaxed and listened to latest releases the young officer brought back from America.

"Rap is nailing music to the mat," she observed.

"It's okay; variety is the spice of life."

One hour later, with shoes left at the door, they squatted on the floor and finished lunch at *Shagalinku*, a popular restaurant. It was a lovely lunch of fried rice, rich with so-called 'particulars' in abundance: peas, baby carrots, pepper, and *halal* meat. The eatery did not serve alcohol. People went there to eat decent meals, not to booze.

Nnénna was glad she came, but his sudden silence was suffocating. "You drove over 40 miles from Kaduna to buy me lunch in Zaria; what's on your mind, Capt'n?"

"Miss Bassey, actually," he said, reminding her how he called Tosina during his first days of knowing her.

"Dagogo, you are not being fair to me. Why pitch me in the middle? If you don't want her, just tell her."

"Do you really... actually think so?"

"I don't want to think. Just make up your mind. Listen, I liked her, and I will hate to see her hurt. I will not want to see you hurt either. There is actually one thing going for you: she is not after your money. She has seen it all; she prefers love. She wants you. You don't know what you want, and that is the trouble with men."

"Do you blame me? You, whom will you marry?"

"We are talking about you, Officer. If you must know, I have no idea."

"Money is ruled out," he said. "What about love?"

"Don't bet on the money. As is the custom, my father will pass on his wealth to his son. I do not understand love. I will not marry Mr. Faith. Okay, I shall marry Mr. Commonsense. Nothing beats good old common sense."

"I want to marry Miss Commonsense too."

"Good! She makes common sense. You have Giles Iké and Zakky Madaki connections in the army. Your commander-in-chief married from same area. Now, if ever you go into politics, southeastern and south-south states will be at your feet. She has Efik and Igbo connections sticking out of her ears. And I shall be there for you."

"Will you?"

"Of course! We are family, remember." Nnénna looked at him as they walked through an open field. Dagogo was not laughing nor smiling at her lighthearted remarks. "Is that what has been bothering you?"

"No... well, yes; I don't want to lose your friendship. You see, I have no sister. I always dreamt I had one. The day I saw you at Zakky's office, I knew I found her: you. I told Zakky. He said you are his niece. I was thrilled. He jokingly told me not to think about it. I told him there was nothing I wanted more in this world than to be your friend. I promised not to go beyond being a good friend."

"I see."

"I told Tosina. The confession must have informed her interest and our eventual moves. Unfortunately, you never took her seriously. She thought you knew about us."

"That's malarkey! You cannot tell that tale to toddlers. Please, let us skip this chapter. I shall be there for you and be your sister, but I cannot do anything about your girlfriend."

"Thank you. Being there for me means being there for her. You may believe it or not, I love her. She thinks her past had everything to do with our recent problems."

"Dagogo, I did not ask. I do not want to know."

"Truth is that you are very much a part of our lives. The moment you cut us off, something in us died. Without your say-so, I cannot marry her."

"I will not submit to emotional blackmail. Come on, let's go." Nnénna dragged him by the hand toward the parked car. "Listen, what you and Tosina did was wrong. Do not try to sugarcoat it. I have forgiven. I promise to be there for both of you: you and Tosina. Let's go."

Some smart salesmen had converted the space between his Honda Prelude and a battered Peugeot 504 into a theatre matinée. Some spectators sat on the boot and bonnet of the car he had just imported from Belgium. He was furious.

A man in his forties was advertising an herbal aphrodisiac guaranteed to give instant erection that persisted for as long as the user—a man—had life left in him. Every adult knew of *magani* (Hausa for 'medicine'). A young man of about 21 was ready for instant demonstration.

Dagogo fished out his keys and activated the alarm. The men sitting on the car saw him approaching with military menace and melted away. He let Nnénna in, went behind the wheel, and sped off leaving a dense trail of dust.

"I wanted to see that," Nnénna giggled.

"No sister of mine is going to watch such a sordid show that debases African male sexuality."

"I heard it works," she insisted.

"Of course it works. Called *'magani burantashi,'* it induces an instant ailment that triggers, as a side effect, an erection the user cannot control."

"You mean priapism?"

"How did you know that?" He was visibly surprised. "Don't tell me: You are a learned lady."

"*Tank* you, Officer!"

"Someone should refine its active ingredients and control the dosage. Trouble is, in this nation, everybody is so busy doing everything nobody does anything."

When Dagogo and Nnénna entered GIZAM Guesthouse later that evening, Tosina was waiting.

"Tosina baby," Nnénna exclaimed as she embraced her surprised ex-girlfriend warmly. "How did you get here?"

"On the wings of love," Tosina said jokingly.

They talked about everything else except the rift in their relationship. Zakky was at home, and his new catch was busy entertaining them. Late evening, Dagogo took the women to a popular nightclub.

Dagogo was paying too much attention to Nnénna. He danced with Tosina once, and that was when Nnénna nudged him. It was obvious they were having a domestic discord and a bigger trouble covering the fact. Nnénna did not want to be in the middle of the brewing brouhaha. When Zakky breezed in, Nnénna complained of a lingering headache. She had had a busy day. She needed to rest her bones. Zakky offered to take Nnénna and his new catch back to the Guesthouse, leaving Dagogo and Tosina to sort out their lives.

The next day, before Zakky woke up, Nnénna asked his driver to take her to the airport. As she settled into the backseat of the car, Tosina ran out of the sitting room.

"Nné, may I have a word?"

She paused, looked back, and said, "Sure, you may." Alone in Tosina's presence, Nnénna felt uncomfortable.

Tosina looked bland as she approached. She stopped a respectable distance from the car and said, "I am not going to ask for forgiveness. What I did is unforgivable, but you are still the only friend I have. These past many months without you hurt like hell. I deserve every minute of the misery and more. Yet, I want to ask you a fat favor: If I ever get married to Dagogo, I want you to be my chief bridesmaid. Wait, if you don't do it for obvious reason, I will understand." As Nnénna began to speak, she interjected again: "Please do not refuse outright; just think about it. Please?"

Nnénna complied. "*Maituki, mu tefi!*"

The Hausa-speaking driver took off as if on a cued horse.

In the plane to Lagos, Nnénna prayed for Dagogo and Tosina to sort out their domestic differences without her. She had had it up to the back of her teeth with them. She liked him, but he had heavy emotional baggage. She will treat him like a normal cousin, nothing more. She understood him; she never wished she had a senior brother, but she sometimes wished there was somebody of the same sex that was close. Her mother, Chināsa, was never there; as a mother, she was a failure driven by circumstances beyond her control.

She sometimes wished there was someone else she could relate to on an equal basis without worrying, when she spoke her mind, whether she ruffled his or her plumage: Someone I will never lose; someone who will not easily get hurt, too hurt to hurt me back badly. I want someone I can trust—even if the person eventually betrays my trust.

Only one person could fill the mold: a twin sister. She came alone to the world, which was good because a double would have changed the entire equation of daughter-father dynamics. She chortled at the thought of a twin sister.

Gilbert was a wonderful father, a fact that more than made up for all other things in life she could not have. She did not want many things out of life; just one friend, male or female, was all she wished she had at that point in her life.

A frequent flyer, she could not recall takeoff. An airhost was passing around some refreshments. She passed. She did not want to lose her train of thought. She was taxing her brain to figure what she really wanted out of life: I need someone to trust; someone to want me; someone to need me; someone to love; someone to love me; someone to love without Carla and Zina in tow; someone to.... There is no competition; no one comes close: That someone is my father.

"Ladies and gentlemen, we are approaching the domestic wing of Murtala Muhammed International Airport, Lagos. Please fasten your seatbelts. In a few moments, we shall commence our descent. The weather on the ground is typical for this time of the year: hot, humid, and hazy."

Nnénna instinctively went for the seatbelt and touched a body. The plane was free boarding. It was half-full when she boarded. She had closed her eyes to rest them and dozed off. Whoever came in later should have found a seat elsewhere. She did not say a word. She did not open her eyes, until the plane landed and taxied slowly to the center of the airport. She opened her eyes slowly.

"Hello, Sleeping Beauty."

"Mr. President!"

"My Campus Queen!"

"What are you doing here?"

"I'm on a business trip," George Offiah responded.

They talked while they disembarked. On the tarmac, they hugged. She was going to Enugu; he was stopping in Lagos. They spent some time at the arrival hall talking and catching up on old times. They both avoided any talks about Tosina.

24

AT THE END OF HER NATIONAL YOUTH SERVICE, Nnénna came back to Enugu. A grand but belated, surprise birthday party awaited her.

"Welcome back to the nest, Mommy love," Gilbert said as Nnénna embraced him.

"I would not say that, Chief Sir Mighty Giles Iké."

Gilbert laughed heartily. Some guests laughed with him, but they did not find her addressing her father thusly funny.

Nnénna had caught the business bug. She was ready to fly. Gilbert let her. She was into international wheeling and dealing while her mates still applied to local law firms. It was a rapid transformation. She soon found incessant travels unnecessary economic wastes. She installed computers, fax machines, and more telephones lines. She organized seminars and professional development workshops for staff members. Steadily, she decentralized decision making and exposed less profitable units that required intensive micromanagement. She convinced her father to dismantle them.

Gilbert took a backseat, spending more time with the family. Since he had time on his hands, he reconsidered the traditional throne of Eziuke. Nnénna vehemently opposed the move because the sudden death of Gilbert's father, Nnanna, might have been a plot to check his rising profile as an in-law of Chimé clan. She did not want his father involved in a dispute that predated his birth and still lingered long after the death of her grandfather. To date, there was still no occupant of the colonial-instituted throne since Eze Okéifè died.

Gilbert agreed to backpedal and wait for Fernando to come of age.

Nnénna could not have accomplished the feat of retiring her father within one year without the assistance of Lora Attah, who had been with Mighty Giles since she graduated from Institute of Management and Technology (IMT) with a diploma in secretarial studies. Lora's proficiency afforded Nnénna the liberty to intensify overseas ventures. Whenever she was in Enugu, everything stayed where she wanted it. Lora was simply irreplaceable.

On a flight back from an overseas trip, Nnénna ran into Frank Obi-Nwaeze at Leonardo da Vinci, Rome. It was spring and Europe was still coping with problems unleashed by the breakup of Soviet block. Frank was thrilled. They talked for hours. He told her that an illness had brought him to Rome with his reverend-mother aunt. He enrolled at the Institute of Pastoral Sociology. After graduating with a first degree in theology and philosophy, he proceeded to Dublin, Ireland, where he obtained a graduate degree in world religions. Back in Rome, he registered for a doctoral degree in canon law. Frank was on his way back to Enugu for a year of field study and pastoral duties before his ordination.

The Nwaeze clan was at the local airport to receive their illustrious son. Down the stairs, he walked with a pretty girl by his side: Finlay.

"Holy Madness!" someone screamed. The young man knew Nnénna; he had heard all about her.

The mere fact that a presumptive priest alighted with a pretty woman by his side surprised others. Frank's father soon noticed that it was the same girl at the center of Frank's unexpected quest for Holy Orders. He was nonplussed.

"Frank, I don't think it is wise for us to stay together. I can see your folks across the barriers," Nnénna whispered and increased her steps across the tarmac toward the arrival hall.

Frank followed her. "My folks are not monsters."

"I didn't say that, but... what a heck, it is your party."

They walked across security barriers. The Nwaeze family flooded him with embraces and good wishes. In the excited commotion and emotive welcome at the airport, Frank made sure Nnénna did not disappear by holding on to the strap of her handbag. To his father, he introduced her as Barrister Nnénna Iké. Chief Judge Francis Obi Nwaeze knew her. Frank explained that they had run into each other in Rome accidentally, which is true. She was kind to have him at their place in Lagos for a couple of hours... actually for four hours. The brief but swift intro sounded reassuring to his parents, especially coming from a prospective priest.

A week later, he visited Nnénna at her Zik Avenue office. Frank wanted to know if they could meet more often "just for old time's sake."

"I don't know if that is wise. I really do not know if any good is going to come out it. Not that I mind, but...."

"You are with a man of God; what more guarantees can anyone ask?"

"I am not asking for guarantees. Frankly, Frank... by the way, should I still call you Frank?"

"Call me Frankie, if you want."

Nnénna blushed and looked at him closely, eyeball to eyeball. "No, Frank is fine. Okay, Frank, why not come to our house and meet with my folks. I'm sure my father will be dying to meet with you at long, long last."

"You think that is wise?"

"Sure. Dad is a knight of the Church you serve, and he is a titled man." She suddenly remembered his convincing phrase and added, "What more guarantees can you ask, Brother?"

"You win, Milady," Frank teased.

Nnénna noticed certain uneasiness and addressed the obvious issue: "Yes, he knows about us. Listen, if you do not feel at home within five minutes, we shall go out and have a meal at Zodiac."

"No, Gemini: it's right in front of the Bishop's residence. I will not want to stray too far away."

"Hmm, it sounds great."

"I'll raise some funds," Frank teased further.

"Please, don't raid church funds for me; it's my treat."

"Whatever you say, I am sold."

"Good. Please, don't put on this immaculate-white alb; it's intimidating and inappropriate."

Frank visited with her family and enjoyed it. He got along with everybody and spent hours playing with Fernando. He became so friendly with the boy he visited thereafter whether Nnénna was in or not, invited to a meal or not. Nnénna told Frank that his white robe fascinated the boy; Frank said his chemistry for children made him a natural for God's work.

One Saturday, Nnénna was at work when her father called to say they were going to the village. Somebody had refused food, as is said of the recently dead, and the funeral was late that afternoon. Could she come back earlier and take Fernando to see Frank? She agreed.

"Néna," Fernando said, "Father Frank came."

"'Nando, he is not a father yet; he's Brother Francis to you, okay?

"No, he is Father Frank."

Nnénna was not going to argue with him. Instead, she summoned the babysitter: "Clara! Please make little Lord Iké decent; we are going to the Seminary. Okay, Almighty Male: go upstairs and get ready."

Fernando stood his ground, apparently not looking at her. "It's Father Frank."

"Okay, whatever. *Fada* Frank it is. Now, go upstairs." As soon as Fernando dashed off, a pair of soft hands gently retrained her head. "Oops!" she said as surprisingly cold hands snuffed out light from her sight. "Who the heavens has these cold but soft palms?"

"Not-yet-Father Frank," he whispered into her ears. Slowly, he let go of his hands. As she pulled away, he held her by the shoulders and said, "Men with warm hearts have soft, cold hands."

Nnénna still had both hands on her face as Frank wheeled her around. She removed her hands and saw Frank grinning like a sophomore. "I wonder what they teach priests these days," she joked. "Welcome. Where were you?" Frank pointed to the large garden at the back. "Oh, experiencing... who's that weird monk that talked to birds... Saint Patrick?"

"To be a monk, you must be weird. That was St Francis of Assisi. Saint Patrick killed snakes in Ireland."

"I thought it was St. Bridget? Never mind. Come and join me; I am starving." Softly, she added, "It seems the mountain has come to Mohammed, but I need some peace."

Frank and Nnénna were in the garden as western clouds rolled over and dimmed sunlight. Golden sunrays lit the sky like a shaded bedside lamp. They talked. Frank wanted some answers "so as not to live a lie," but Nnénna was not forthcoming.

"Nnénna, I need to know," he pleaded.

She did not consider certain aspects of her life any of his business, and she told him matter-of-factly: "Frank, you are not my father; I don't owe you any explanation."

"I really want to know what happened. Was it what you wanted, or did it just happen?"

"Oh my God... for goodness sake, that was ages ago. By the way, what was the coma all about? I picked up the gist from some chick the other day, a bona fide blabbermouth."

He told her the story. It was still very fresh in his mind. He looked at Nnénna constantly, and he paused severally. Apparently, he had not fully recovered.

"You silly boy," Nnénna said. "Did you see any fin on me when I undressed?"

He shook his head.

"You did not notice my fishtail until Carla told you, right? What made you believe that crap for a moment?"

"I am sorry."

"I don't mind; it was not me who went into a coma. It should not have pushed you into priesthood anyway; for goodness sake, it does not suit you."

"You reckon?"

"Well, who am I to preach. If God calls you, answer. However, my deduction is that you felt you have to atone for some sin. Your dad did not help either."

"Well, it's late now. My father lost his £1000.00 bet with Zina's dad."

"He did not. It ended in an out-of-court settlement." She told Frank how she went to the Club with her father. It was on the eve of Tony Ikpeama's departure to London for Zina's wedding. They brought it up and, as Frank's father was about to issue a check for £1,500.00, she elected to defend him for a 25% commission. It was a simple case: Frank was not yet ordained. Technically, he was still available. Tony could not plead her dalliance with Frank; she could strike below the belt with a secret of which not even Gilbert knew.

"You defeated my godfather, Tony Ikpeama, SAN?"

"I stood very tall. I made mincemeat of two legal experts. You should have seen Daddy. His eyes were saying, 'Show them, my girl.' Well, your dad did hand over the check: a gift for the bride. Say, did you have plans to respect the bet?"

"I guess. Zina and I discussed it. We decided to lead our separate lives and, if after our graduation we felt strongly about it, we could put a smile on their faces."

"Oh my God!"

"What?"

"Nothing," she said abruptly to conceal her feeling. The full weight of Zina's outburst hit her like a wet bag of sand.

She brushed it off her mind and said, "Now, it is too late to worry; she is married."

"To Tee Jay Dangoya of all people. He should have been shot for the way he used and dumped girls."

"Hey, Mr. Priest, don't judge."

"I'm not judging, but a good Catholic chick marrying a Muslim mouse like Tee Jay means that the world is standing on its head."

"That is a terrible thing to say, Frank. Be fair. Forget that my Grandpa is a Muslim; some of our men should get girls from the other sides. That way, we shall nurture the elusive Nigerian nation."

"I'm out of the equation." He spread his hands, showing he was not in contention and masking his irritated demeanor.

"No thanks to Carla. By the way, what happened to pretty Miss Olisa and her brother... your friend, Carl?"

"Ah, Miss Carla Frankenstein was last seen in Holland. Carl is in Abuja. He works with a foreign construction firm. We are still friends. It seems like ages ago. Tell me, Finlay, did you ever intend to forget about us?"

"Frank, what am I supposed to say to you? By the way, 'Finlay' is no more; stay with Nnénna, please."

"*Mea culpa, mea culpa, mea maxima culpa; Ideo precor....*"

"Whatever that means, its sounds good to my ears."

"It's an apology of sorts."

"My dear, I am Catholic—born and bred; I studied a romance language—French—at Queen's; and I studied law."

"Thanks for the reminder. Now, tell me: what about us?"

"What? You will go back to the peace and quiet of senior seminary and expect me to sit here and think about us? What is that supposed to mean? Okay, I will give it straight to you, Frank: You took my innocence. You made me a woman. I am not joking. Now, bend down your ears and prepare to hear some real iniquities. Are you ready, Padre Francesco?"

Frank nodded and said smilingly, "Speak, my child, for God who sees all forgives all."

"Good. Please forgive me Father Francis for I have sinned exceedingly. I broke the sixth commandment. You made me feel dirty, Father, especially as you abandoned me on top of an ad-hoc altar of wooden desks like a cow carcass on a slaughterhouse slab. Was I supposed to be a sacrificial lamb… to wash away your sins? Tell me."

Frank held her as she laughed loudly, looked into her eyes, and planted a kiss squarely on her lips. Nnénna did not need any encouragement. She had worked herself up, and she loved it. She gave as much as she got.

"Let's go," she said as they came up for air.

Frank followed meekly. Her parents had come back, but she did not want him to say hello to them. She was toying with his emotions. The earlier she got him off her hair, the better for both of them. She pulled out an ageing family car and drove him across town to Uwāni section.

She said nothing as she negotiated the evening traffic. Frank let her be. At the senior seminary gate, he disembarked and said, "Good night, my dear sister. Tell Fernando I'll bring that picture book tomorrow."

"Are you sure?"

"Yes." As someone approached, Frank lowered his voice: "Don't worry about tonight; it won't happen again. I have no regrets, though." Raising his voice, he said, "Good night, sister, and God bless you." He turned and walked through the gate. He was poised, but a big bag of bewilderment trailed him to the rickety gate of Bigard Memorial Seminary.

"Good night, Brother Francis," Nnénna mumbled as the sweet sound of benediction drifted to her ears. The Gregorian chant was so soothingly smooth and striking she stayed.

Adoremus in aeternum sanctissimum Sacramentum.

Laudate Dominum omnes gentes: laudate eum omnes populi.

At Kenyatta Market junction, she waited for the lights. Lying where Frank had sat was a leather-bound book. She wanted to make a U-turn. She knew his dorm and the room number, but why would a lone young woman go asking for a reverend in a senior seminary and at night?

At College Road Supermarket, opposite Campus gate, she stopped to buy something with which to pacify Fernando for 'taking *Fada* Frank away.' She took the book with her. For all she knew, it might be a personal present from His Holiness the Pope or a priceless prize. It was wrong to lead one chosen by the Lord to a sinful kiss, but she had no regrets. She was paying for sweets and ice creams when a note fell off from the book. She quickly picked it up. Her name was on it.

The moment Nnénna got in, her father noticed an antithesis of the sendoff night. Fernando had reported her to Gilbert, their father, and followed it up with complaints: "Néna took *Fada* Frank away," he kept saying.

She was all over her father, jostling childishly with touchy Fernando, who wanted her punished. Gilbert intervened, told Nnénna to apologize, and urged Fernando to accept the gifts. He refused the bribe. He wanted Gilbert to scold and spank Nnénna. Fernando was not getting his way, so he went over to Mom. At that age, Fernando knew Chināsa and Nnénna did not normally get along. Nnénna followed him, imploring him to accept the sweets. Chināsa ignored them.

Nnénna just wanted to have fun. She was happy. She was using Fernando's silliness to exhibit her ecstasy. She did not let go until Fernando was ready for bed. Gilbert was thrilled by the juvenile antics and more thrilled when she announced a work-free Sunday. They will worship together at Holy Ghost Cathedral and then come back to wait for Frank. The prospect of meeting Frank within a specified period settled Fernando's fretfulness. He accepted the sweets and went upstairs to Nnénna's bedroom.

As Nnénna lay in bed that night, words from the poem kept ringing in her ears. Silly Frank, she sighed, religious romanticism must have confused him to the point of thinking that he can binge on no-water-added palm wine on Saturday night and proclaim sobriety on Sunday morning. She knew men could be as immature as you want them to be. She knew that there is something strange about this thing called love: In her books, love is a sudden attraction between strangers that forces them to eject reason from the realm of reality, a mild madness that is dangerously delirious.

Nnénna said her prayers, brought out the poem, and read it again to herself:

I don't want to lose you
The affection endeared in abundance
The sincerity of our college romance
Yes, I fear I might lose you.

You mean so much to me
Simply put, the very best
Fondness
Kindness
Undoubted

You have been so good to me
Yes, the very best
Cheerfully
Thoughtfully
Undaunted

I don't want to lose you
Reassured, I am still afraid of the future
I fear that something might rupture
I fear that I might lose you.

He loved her; undoubtedly, he was still in love, and he was undaunted by the constraints of coming clerical concerns. Though immersed in Catholicity, Nnénna could simplify and separate the concepts of celibacy and chastity. She will have him as a friend even after his ordination, a true friend. She will understand his vocation more and help him to achieve his goals. She did not know how to achieve her wish without ruffling the currents of Coal City community, but she will do her best to help him and be there for him. She will kiss him again and recreate the scene of seven years before, if it will take the recreation and much more to be Frank's friend.

At the base of her soul, she knew the answer to her worries was in four simple words: I am in love. At last, she found that particular someone she always wanted: a friend and a confidant who will never hurt her even if he wanted.

She turned on her right side to succumb to the soothing solace of *Somnus*, the harvesting hallow of *Hypnos*, and the ensuing embrace of aura of *Ụra*–the sibling of death in Igbo theosophy. The harmonious early-evening Gregorian chant of benediction of the Blessed Sacrament from Bigard Memorial Seminary still played in her head:

Tantum ergo Sacramentum
Veneremur cernui:
Et antiquum documentum
Novo cedat ritui:
Praestet fides supplementum
Sensuum defectui.

Genitori, Genitoque
Laus et iubilatio,
Salus, honor, virtus quoque
Sit et benedictio:
Procedenti ab utroque
Compar sit laudatio.
Amen.

When next Frank called and met Nnénna at home, she found his knowledge of Latin very captivating. He could say and sing all popular church prayers and songs in Latin before he entered university. When he studied Latin in Rome, it was easy to fill in the grammatical blanks. She walked Nnénna through the basics by breaking down known phrases from *Oremus* ('Let us pray') to *Credo in unum Deum* of the Nicene Creed. Of course, she knew to say the Litany of Virgin Mary in Latin from elementary school.

Frank knew the story behind every chant. For example, he explained to her that *Tantum Ergo* is actually the last two stanzas from *Pange Lingua* ('Sing, my tongue'), a poem by St. Thomas Aquinas for the Solemnity of Corpus Christi.

To awaken further her interest in Latin and to move away from heavy-duty theology that could be off-putting at times, Frank taught her to sing *Gaudeamus Igitur*. He also gave her a rough rendition of the lyrics in English. "Touted as the oldest song to reveal the carefree campus life of medieval students, it is still a permanent musical treat at graduation ceremonies of many European universities."

"I suspect seminaries here don't use it, if the lyrics really convey decadence of centuries-old campus life."

"You are right, my dear, but I see nothing wrong with wishing long life to all voluptuous virgins that are easy and beautiful, and to mature women who are still tender, lovable, and hardworking."

"You don't, huh," she said, sounding serious.

"No," he offered and smiled. "Well, it did not feature at my graduation. Remind me to give you a tape of Johannes Brahms in his Academic Festival Overture, *Opus 80*… I guess he composed it in 1880. You will love it."

"I am not into classical music. Anything outside Ludwig van Beethoven's Symphony No. 5 is old Deutsch to me; but, sincerely speaking, I sure look forward to this number 80."

25

MIDYEAR OPENED THE FLOODGATE. SUITABLE and unsuitable suitors came from home, abroad, and everywhere in-between. Any man of means looking for a bride gave her a thought. Many made inquiries. Some followed up leads and fell by the wayside; very few made it to her court. To some suitors, every person remotely related to her became an avenue to her presence.

Going through Zakky had since become a cul-de-sac. Besides, if Nnénna wished to marry a military man, he proved to be a bad ambassador. Gilbert was not available for family-to-family proposals that matchmakers favored. He washed his hands before the middleperson worked out how to crack coconut without splitting the shell.

"You are better off talking to her," Gilbert advised. "Or, better still, you may want to tell the young man to talk to her. Here at home or at work, I won't be in the way."

Some took up the challenge. One was in the United States. His family asked him to visit and see for himself. He did. He met her for lunch at Modotels, located in the business district of the city. The young man went on about himself for so long he bored even himself.

Nnénna decided to cut him down to size. "Do you have any of these degrees with you?" She was no village Veronica; she had degrees too.

"That's not nice, if I may say so," he declared.

"Sure, you may say so; it is still a free country. You see, sunny boy, three degrees don't make a marriage." She called for the bill, signed it, and wished him a safe flight back to Houston or 'Who sent you,' as Lora dubbed it.

Another Americana breezed into her office the next week dripping hair spray, oozing a strong masculine perfume, and brandishing his 'Green Card'—the United States' Permanent Resident Card—and tens of fancy plastic cards. Once he sat down, it was *gonna-gerrit* galore. She restrained herself from laughing at the American street speak of a homegrown and cassava-fed Coal City boy.

"Okay, Charlie boy, may I put in a word?"

"Feel free-e! See, in Uncle Sam's God's own country...."

"Do you mind?" She was losing her patience.

"Sure, sure.... Hit me! Shoot, baby."

"Thank you. Is your divorce through?"

He recoiled. "You say what?"

Nnénna cleared her throat and tried to imitate the gay gesticulations of her visitor. "Hey, I ain't gonna give no crazy Americana my butt to whop; gerrit, huh?"

The man knew when to quit. Lora the secretary came in as he left and helped Nnénna to a satisfying laugh.

A week after, some bloke phoned her from Liverpool. He asked her to fly out and meet him in London, so they could talk. It was his first and last call Lora forwarded to Nnénna. The chap called daily for two weeks thereafter. The last time, he wanted to talk business, 'super deals.' Lora called him a 429-ner, a foreign faceless fraud preying on people.

Gilbert laughed whenever Nnénna told him stories of her encounters with suitors. Chināsa did not find them funny. She feared Nnénna ending up as a sister-wife with whom she cannot compete fairly, since Gilbert let her have it her way. Father and daughter ignored her, as usual. Chināsa and Gilbert stayed home most days and traveled weekends, yet the few evenings he and Nnénna spent together troubled her.

"FEN is no longer a little girl, you know," she said to Gilbert as they cuddled in bed.

"Oh, she is now a big woman? Good news!"

NNÉNNA: MY DAUGHTER, MY MOTHER

Chināsa decided to do something about Nnénna's marital status, if only to get her out of the house and reclaim all evenings with her husband. She called Fanny.

Fanny told her to consider it done. She became a self-appointed middleperson to avoid any missteps. Within the week, she found a perfect match. The potential husband, a distant relation of a friend and a university graduate, was doing well in the booming business of public relations and politics. He was a surefire candidate for political office. His single status stopped his contesting in the last primaries. Fanny figured that a picture-perfect partner with all the right connections was the juice needed to power his politics.

Chināsa conspired with Fanny to soften the plot with a surprise birthday party. Thrilled by the prospect of success, she thanked Fanny profusely and confided in her husband. The plot leaked out within hours of her asking Gilbert for money. Nnénna traveled to Lagos for the week.

Fanny went back to the drawing board. She planned a big bash the following week for a federal minister. Nnénna told everyone, including her mother who had become too friendly lately, that she was very busy. She hated parties, and she will be of little help to anybody in the select, senior crowd. Fanny went ahead anyway and planned the party. Nnénna got an invitation card and told company secretary Lora to send a case of fine wines and a note of heartfelt regrets.

Fanny was furious. She called the house a day after the party and asked to speak with Nnénna.

"FEN, it's your godmother," Chināsa called out.

"I am not in," Nnénna mouthed.

Chināsa rattled on after offering that Nnénna must have gone to bed. She played along because Nnénna was rocking Fernando to sleep, and she did no want to ruffle her feathers. She replaced the receiver after thirty minutes.

"Why won't you talk to her?"

"I've nothing to say to the busybody."

"You can't talk about Fanny like that, young lady."

"I just did. She should find a husband for herself first. Now, can I go and wash my mouth?" Nnénna was no longer in the mood to pussyfoot. She wanted no part of the sudden and annoying interference from Fanny of all people.

"Use an entire bar of soap," Chināsa yelled.

Gilbert smiled as Nnénna got up, winked, and lifted Fernando off the sofa. She walked up the stairs to her bedroom with the sleeping big bundle. Lately, Fernando refused to sleep alone in his bedroom, so he now slept in Nnénna's bedroom.

"You are unbelievable, you... just like your father," Chināsa continued. Turning to Gilbert, she asked, "Do you know why she suddenly hates her with a passion?"

"Search me," he replied with a smug smile.

"You two don't fool me. Go ahead... share not your little secrets. When it bursts, I pick up the pieces. This time, I am not going to wait. I will find out. I do not know a single thing Fanny has done wrong in this family. Did you ever tell your daughter that she owes Fanny her life? Without Fanny's friendship, where would I be today?"

Chināsa met with Fanny within the week. Fanny admitted noticing Nnénna's coldness. She must have given her the impression that she was having an affair with Gilbert. Nothing like that happened, she assured Chināsa. That was comforting because Chināsa had also thought they were at it, but fighting Fanny over the coziness with her husband could have caused unnecessary consternation, injected needless domestic discord, and ruined their friendship. That Nnénna was seemingly fighting for her mother impressed Chināsa.

Suddenly, pride in Nnénna dried up as Chināsa drove home. She believed that Nnénna was fighting her own wars. Nnénna accepted her and her husband—they are her parents;

Fanny was an outsider, an intruder. Chināsa did not believe her interest was at stake here because the bond between father and daughter was too strong and inflexible.

Chināsa apologized to Nnénna that evening and called for a truce. "You might not have been born without her help. I really owe her a lot."

"So much so you were willing to allow her to walk all over your domain? It smacks of inferiority complex."

"FEN, we don't always achieve our goals by fighting. Imagine what I could have done without having the facts, and it is not true. Please do me this favor: Stop giving her a hard time." With tears in her eyes, Chināsa went on to tell Nnénna the sordid story of her life to drive home her points.

Nnénna felt for her mother. "It's all right, Mom. If that is what you want, I shall do me best. One thing though, she must stop trying to match-make me. She is my godmother, not my god. My private life is my business, full stop!"

Fanny flatly refused to give up. Whenever she wanted something badly, she got it. Chināsa hinted her that a surefire avenue was their uncle Chief Chimé. Within a week, the chief was in Fanny's camp. He phoned Gilbert and asked him over to his house in New Haven area of Enugu. It did not take much formality to introduce the meat of the meeting.

"I have checked out the family; they are clean."

"It's not me they want to marry," Gilbert protested.

"Correct, but I don't like the tone of your voice."

Gilbert apologized.

"I just want you to know before they come to knock on the door; that is, to make initial inquiries."

"I know what 'knocking on the door' means, Uncle. You must understand the amount of peer pressure I am sitting on. I have told my friend Manny Eze that I will not force Nnénna into any marriage. He says I am not serious."

"*Eh hee...* are you? Never mind, go ahead."

"Chināsa says I want to keep her at home. Whatever for; am I going to marry Nnénna, my daughter… my mother? I don't understand Chināsa these days; I really don't."

"Great men did not understand them, so just stop trying. It is so bad our sages say that the man who a woman does not kill dies his destined death."

Gilbert continued, ignoring the obvious sexiest statement: "What does Chināsa want me to do? We are enjoying so much free time together because Nnénna has taken over and retired me. Yet she is not happy to see her own daughter on the few evenings and weekends she is at home. She thinks I empower her to reject men."

"Do you?"

"Uncle, believe me, I won't talk to her or the lucky young man about their coming and their going. What I have said to Nnénna is that I will talk to the lucky man on her wedding day. I will tell him about Mama. I will remind him that if Nnénna sheds a teardrop… just a drop, I will come after him with all my might and my money. Nnénna has agreed."

"It sounds fair to me," Chimé nodded. When something touched on his late sister, Gilbert's mother, they both shared the same intensity of emotion.

"Do you want to know what I will say?"

"You don't dissipate the desire to defecate by farting."

"Yes, our ancestors were right: Farting does not disperse the urge to defecate; its fragrance merely foretells the taste of 'Mr. Big Stuff'!" He cracked a smile, caught himself, and sat up. "I take it then that I should make just one big splash."

"Right," Chimé retorted, showing disinterest in the silly defilement of his apt proverb. In Igbo rules of etiquette, no one explains proverbs; you figure out the meaning. "By the way, does it mean that the exploratory visit should proceed?"

"As our Owere brethren say, *Ụyọ wụ ụyọ mụ 'a gị*—the house is our house."

26

IT WAS EARLY AUGUST. THE RAINY SEASON WAS taking its seasonal break. Nnénna had traveled abroad on a business trip. She came back on the first flight from Lagos. An exploratory delegation was coming for the first formal rite of matrimony: *ikụakanụzọ* ('knocking on the door'). Nnénna wished she had stayed back in London, but she knew Chief Chima Chimé would never forgive the slight, even though her presence was not strictly required.

She slept in Enugu that Friday night. The prospect of an arranged marriage preoccupied her. It was strange, but she agreed to play along. She was not moving into any man's house any time soon. Nothing will be certain for many more moons. She had a firm to run; no man will change the fact for at least two solid years. The relationship between her and Gilbert marveled many, but she did not care to know who became king of the Igbo and made them lords.

Saturday, she left before noon. At the Ninth Mile Corner, she turned onto the old Enugu-Onitsha road leading to Udi. After Monarch Breweries was the junior seminary in Nsude. Frank was teaching there as part of his preordination work. At a moment's impulse, she swerved sharp right onto the dusty road to the immaculate school compound. Suddenly, she heard loud screams and screech of tires. She looked at her rearview mirror and saw a group of people pointing at her. She stopped.

"*I can drive!*" the bus driver's assistant shouted.

"Stupid woman driver," a female passenger yelled.

"It's yourself you will kill," another woman cursed.

Nnénna backed up, got out of her truck, and asked to know why they were picking on her. Everyone was talking at the same time. She let them babble, her eyes defiant behind designer sunglasses. Finally, the driver explained.

"It was God that saved you... and everybody here. You didn't *trafficate*, and you... we were coming with speed."

"We nearly smashed you," another passenger added.

From what she gathered and recollected, she reckoned that she had an attention lapse. She passed the bus while the driver bribed the police at a checkpoint. It was a long way up the hill. They must have been tailgating her. She apologized and offered to pay for any inconveniences. The offer brought a storm of insults: Is she trying to buy our lives? Is that how her sugar daddy made the money to buy her a four-wheel drive? Who does she think she is? Is she Queen Elizabeth?

Nnénna apologized again. She told them that she had a lot on her mind. They listened and calmed down. She gave the driver her card and requested him to send her the cost of incident-related faults. "Oh, by the way, the car is my father's company car. He will readily tell any of you that this is truly out of character."

The driver, a young man of about 25, could not believe his eyes. *Mighty Giles International*, he whistled. He knew her father; his money bought the bus for Nicholas, the bus owner. A wave of whispering and whimpering floated across the bus of sardine-packed heads. They knew she was supposed to be at home for the traditional engagement ritual: What is she doing out here? Why didn't we recognize her? Rural people love juicy gossips; Nnénna set off a nuclear brand.

"My daughter, may God bless you in your journeys," an older woman offered. Her son had benefited from Gilbert's scholarship programs for indigent but intelligent students.

"Thank you, Ma'am. If it will help," Nnénna offered, "I will ask a reverend father to thank God for journey mercies."

Frank was delighted to see Nnénna. He had just finished brunch. They went to the chapel. He offered prayers and glorified God, as she had promised.

They strolled past the classrooms and found a plank nailed over two stomps under a cashew tree.

"You know this guy?" Frank asked.

"I've seen him," Nnénna giggled.

"Seen? Are you sure you want to marry him?"

"Yes, *seen*—not slept. Frank, what is this, catechism?"

"Stop being difficult; you wanted to talk. The last thirty minutes have been like getting a cup back from a baboon...."

"To whom you didn't have to give a cup of water?"

"I didn't say that. Come on, smile for me." He held her hand and shook her. She smiled. "That's my girl."

"Okay, I don't know. I don't know if I want to marry. As the ritual drags on, and everyone is off my Daddy's back, we shall see. If it works, fine; if not, fine too."

"Let me get something straight: You are not ready for marriage. You agreed to this because it will drag on and keep all the other bees off your royal hive. Most importantly, you will ease the pressure on your father. You are not thinking about yourself; it is all about your Daddy? This thing surely deserves its own name in psychology: *Nnénna Complex*."

"Stop, Frank; I don't want to talk about my Daddy."

"Okay, come here... come... close your eyes. Relax." Frank took off her glasses and massaged the sides of her eyes until her breathing steadied. He knew her nerves were on edge. She was not thinking straight. "Okay, Ms. Managing Director of Mighty Giles International Limited, it's time to go."

Nnénna looked at the time. "Oh my God, how time flies. You think I should leave now?"

"That's the general idea, my dear; but, first, we must pray and ask God to take charge and be in control henceforth."

"You think I need prayers, huh?"

"Oh, you need prayers every time and every day. Always PUSH: Pray until something happens." Frank placed his hands on her head and said a short prayer, asking God to send down his angels to be with her. "And may the Almighty Father guard and guide you through these difficult times and all the days of your life, one God forever and ever.... Amen?"

"Amen!" As he walked her to the 4x4, she asked, "Are you sure you don't want to come with me?"

"Yes. I shall come to the final ritual of wine-carrying ceremony...."

"*Ịgbankwụ* is a long way down the road. You will get the Holy Orders by then and officiate at the wedding."

"No way! Your father will settle for His Lordship the Bishop only because His Holiness the Pope will not come to town for a wedding." They laughed. "Here is the cassette I promised you. Drive carefully. Do not worry about a thing. Come and see me whenever you like."

"You know I will." Nnénna turned and wanted to hug him. She saw a group of boys in white shirts and khaki shorts. She paused as they passed and saluted Frank respectfully as if he were already ordained. Then she held him. "You know you are the only guy I trust to be with without his dreaming of taking me to bed and doing things to me."

"I don't know about that," he said and hugged her. He looked around and gently pushed her away.

"Sorry, Holy Ghost fire carried me away." Before Frank could caution her against blasphemy, she moved on to mundane matters. "Why don't we have lunch on Monday? I'll tell you all about the outcome of events at home."

"I have classes all day on Monday... and I can't stay out late because Tuesday is a busy day. What of Wednesday?"

"I shall ask Lora to clear my to-do list and send one of the drivers to pick you up."

27

THE DELEGATES CAME EARLIER THAN NNÉNNA had anticipated. The Lodge was in a clean-and-tidy condition. When she drove in, children came rushing to the gate to catch a glimpse of her. She waved and called some by their names. She alighted and apologized for not buying them market stuff. *Hakuna matata*; local shops were open. She parted with a fistful of cash.

Gilbert came to meet her. "Are you okay, Mommy?"

"Sure. I went to see Frank. He sends his regards."

"Good. Come in. Just be yourself and do not offer your hand unless they do. A little knee bending...."

"Daddy! "

"You know I am not enjoying this. Just say the word and we shall cut off all these ceremonies."

"It's not my making; blame your Uncle Chima, the chief."

She saw the men seated in their large sitting room. She knew they came with everything they could get. She walked into the large living room, greeted politely, apologized for her lateness, and excused herself to put away her bag. There was no bag; she needed time to think things over properly and to catch her breath. Nnénna did not ask after her mother and Fernando; they were having so much fun, as if they could not wait to marry her off to the next available single male.

They were about to get down to business when Nnénna walked back into the room and asked the suitor to come with her. She did not stop to look at astonished faces. She walked out. The suitor got up slowly, gauged some facial expressions, and looked at the arranged-marriage mastermind. From the family corner, Fanny flicked her head encouragingly.

Nnénna was waiting under the broad-leaved umbrella tree at the far end of the forecourt of The Lodge.

"Hi," he said, smiling uneasily.

"Hi? George Offiah, is that all you can say? *Hi?*"

"Nnénna, please, I know this is weird, but I believe it is the only way to prove to you that I am really serious."

"Serious? Are you really serious?"

"You know you are special...."

"George, cut that crap, or the whole charade is over now."

"Nné, please, don't do this to me. I have always admired you and.... Okay, I could not drop Tosina without rocking your friendship. You did not think I was going to marry her?"

"Hold it there: Why not?"

"You see...."

"I don't see anything. I consider her family and a friend. Badmouthing her will not do any good. Let us talk about us. You saw me at her wedding. Why didn't you say something? You couldn't phone to tell me about this, yet I awarded you a lucrative but needless publicity contract recently."

"I came to the wedding to see you and talk about us. You were the chief bridesmaid. All eyes were on you. You stole the show. You were the star."

She smiled and said, "Why didn't you tell me then? You were busy handing out your golden cards and sealing deals."

"I am sorry, Nnénna."

"Come on, did you have to wheel out all these guys: Monsignor Eze and Chief Chimé, I understand, but those two northern senators with Senator Arinze and the rest of them? This is supposed to be the exploratory visit."

"I am so sorry. The senators are my political godfathers. You know, when you want something very badly and you ask for some advice, you get plenty."

"And you chose that of your sugar mommy?"

"Who.... What?" George was shaking.

"Fanny, my godmother. Relax, nobody expects you to be a virgin. If you really want us to marry, it could work; but there is a load of lies to sort through. George, stop fidgeting. Believe me, I am no Bimbo Braimoh. She was good for your PR programs. Tosina was there because you needed a mature, inexpensive, and no-risk shoulder to lean on soon after your campus presidential project crash-landed. I am not going to fit into your political pursuits. I hate politics, and partisan politics runs my stomach. I won't be of much help."

"Okay, I have been brash, but I never disrespected you on campus. I am not here with all these people for the fun of it. Forget politics, I am the one involved. Or, are you holding me responsible for those wild days on campus?"

"No, I just detest being Fanny's reward for the bedroom services you render to her. Look, George, I like you. You are a nice person. I did not come to many LAVIC events because Tosina would have come with me. If I had come, my Daddy would have recognized you. Don't worry; you were not the only toy boy she took to LAVIC shows. What I am saying is that you may be doing this for all the wrong reasons."

"I don't think so," he protested. "I cannot be used."

"Listen to me: This is all part of Fanny's bigger plan. If I were close to her, a God-fearing godchild, she will not be working so hard to get you to marry me. She is roping us into her flight of fancy. Unless you know where you are coming from, the future is going to be bleak. I have got Mighty Giles tied up; there are no leaks, believe me."

"Nné, I am not a part of her plans. She's just helping."

Nnénna knew that Fanny had set him up in business and that Gilbert helped her. She knew that Fanny had her eyes set on getting a piece of Mighty Giles. However, divulging the dark details of Fanny's intimate liaisons and business schemes was pointless. George did not deny that they had an affair, and there was no point in pushing the issue.

"You don't know me. You cannot now name my favorite soft drink. Okay, if you want us to go ahead, be prepared to take whatever you see. A note of caution, if you proceed with this, it will not be over until the wedding day. And there may not be a wedding."

George looked lost. "What do you mean?"

"I am afraid it will take hours to explain. I have told you enough to help you make up your own mind. Whatever you decide, I'll go along and make all those big men happy."

"I still don't get it. What do I do?"

"We shall go in there. We shall make everyone happy. We shall all depart happily. We, you and I, shall talk about this at a future date, get to know ourselves, and do this thing for us. There will be no more middlepersons, no more stories told. Now, let us not keep them waiting and guessing. If you really know what you want, you will know what to do."

George's mind flashed back to all the stories he had heard about Nnénna on and off campus. He knew all about Frank's grief and the *Finelay* fable. He called the talks 'trash' but, on a second thought, Frank was a living proof that she might be the fire in all that smoke. He shook his head, put his hands in his pockets to dry his sweating palms, and walked behind Nnénna back to the main building.

As they walked back to the house, Fanny came out from a side door. Nnénna increased her footsteps to get in before she caught up with her outside.

"FEN," Fanny called out, keeping her voice low. She was the only other person who called Nnénna 'FEN'—a pathetic imitation of her friend Chināsa, Nnénna's mother.

"What?" Nnénna demanded without looking at her.

"What is happening?"

"Nothing!" She walked on without looking back.

Fanny looked at George askance. He smiled smugly, clenching and crushing his teeth.

Nnénna was driving back to Enugu after attending church service in Eziuke. At the junior seminary, she wanted to drive in and see Frank, but she decided otherwise. It will not be appropriate to visit on a Sunday afternoon while he might be having lunch with the resident superior. To make the lonely drive down to Enugu enjoyable, she played the cassette Frank gave her. Four stanzas of <u>Gaudeamus Igitur</u> were her favorite.

As a Catholic exposed to the chants of Latin high mass, and with her background in legal education and Frank's Latin lessons, she was able to construct a custom translation of the verses, though she sang the Latin lyrics, repeating the first two lines and the last line as is the tradition:

Gaudeamus igitur,	Let us therefore rejoice,
Juvenes dum sumus;	While we are young;
Post jucundum juventutem,	After a blissful childhood,
Post molestam senectutem	After a miserable adulthood
Nos habebit humus.	The earth will house us.
Vita nostra brevis est,	Our life is short,
Brevi finietur;	It will shortly end;
Venit mors velociter,	Death comes quickly,
Rapit nos atrociter;	Steals us atrociously;
Nemini parcetur.	No one is spared.
Vivat academia,	Long live academia,
Vivant professores,	Long live professors,
Vivat membrum quodlibet,	Long live every male student,
Vivat membra quaelibet;	Long live every female student;
Semper sint in flore!	May they always flourish!
Alma Mater floreat,	May our Alma Mater thrive,
Quae nos educavit;	The source of our education;
Caros et commilitones,	Friends and colleagues all,
Dissitas in regiones,	Wherever they are overall,
Sparsos, congregavit.	Heed her invitation.

By the time she entered the city limits, she still wanted to keep her head clear of everything that transpired on Saturday and thereafter. She tried a mental translation of the chant into commonwealth Igbo, also called '*Igbo izugbe.*' It was a tough-going proposal, but she decided to do it anyway.

On reaching home, she got a glass of water, walked over to the studio, and started with her favorite *Vivat academia* stanza. Before her parents drove in, she had a pop rhyme:

    Chiukwu gozie mahadum,
    Chi gozie ndinkuzi dum,
    Chi gozie ụmụakwụkwọ dum,
    Ma nwoke ma nwaanyị dum;
    Ka ha niile dị mgbe dum!

It reminded her of a kindergarten song in honor of teachers:

Anyị agbasago akwụkwọ	We are done with schooling
Anyị agbasago akwụkwọ	We are done with schooling
Ekene dịrị ndinkuzi	Thanks be to the teachers
Kuziere anyị akwụkwọ!	Who taught us!
Ekene dịrị ndinkuzi	Thanks be to the teachers
Kuziere anyị akwụkwọ!	Who taught us!

Nnénna succeeded in repressing the tormenting thoughts of unnecessary pressures from marriage managers. Her father was of little help lately. He had become so conciliatory with the overbearing overtures of Chief Chima Chimé she no longer trusted his Pontius Pilate position. She wished she could fast-forward Wednesday, when she will meet Frank and let it all out to his listening ears. His usual understanding and strong support will soothe my soul, she concluded.

Two months later, Nnénna missed her menstrual period for the second time in her life. She was definitely pregnant. She knew it, and she was not going to stress about it. She dreamt of a beautiful baby, a baby girl she will call Obiagæli Akunna, in anticipation of her plans to spoil Grandma on her third coming with 'the wealth of her father' (*akụ nna ya*).

28

INSIDE CITY CATHOLIC CATHEDRAL, INVITEES SAT. Anyone who was big and relevant in the city was there. Business associates flew in for the very special occasion. They came from the East and from the West. They came from Kafanchan-Kaduna-Kano-Katsina-Kaura Namoda axis. Madaki came with his retinue of friends on a private plane. Members of LAVIC flew in on a chartered flight. Now retired General Yerima Sambo-Razaq had arrived the previous week. Regular flights brought in more men and women of timber and caliber, the shakers and quakers of military, political, and socioeconomic setups. Every room in the city's five-star hotels was booked for the weekend. It was like a colorful annual convention of the ruling political party.

Many religious groupings vied for vantage positions. All were color-coordinated and dressed to surpass the others. Catholic knights in ceremonial costumes competed with judges in long robes. Lawyers with wigs and gowns of all shapes and shades complemented seminarians and convent sisters. The brothers of St. Francis wore their brown habits. The Sisters of Our Lady of Fatima shined in their immaculate whites and long black-bead chaplets. Members of Legion of Mary and of Saint Anthony's Guild toned down the colorful laity in coordinated *ashoebi*, society uniform attires.

Admission into the Cathedral was restricted to invitees. An army of overzealous churchwardens easily identified and unceremoniously threw out gatecrashers, though there were neither drinks nor food at this stage of the all-day celebration of the sacrament of matrimony.

It was past the stated start time. No one expected the service to start within the hour. It was not a question of the bride keeping the bridegroom waiting; it was simply the national sense of timing: the so-called 'African time.' The guests were not in a hurry. The day was for a very special occasion; nothing else mattered. The Bishop will take less than one hour to seal the matrimonial union, make a fancy speech about family and God, and collect cold cash for the Church. Thereafter, the trading of ideas, soliciting of personal and political alliances, and sealing of deals will begin.

An hour later, Gilbert walked up the aisle. He was not with the bride. Everyone froze. The thought of a cancellation did not bear entertaining. He walked on as the sea of shades of faces looked up anxiously. He stopped by the front pew, whispered into the groom's right ear, and walked on to the smaller side sacristy. The smartly suited man followed him in quick steps to the chapel. Murmurs of apprehension filled the Cathedral. No one appeared to know what was happening. Rumors were rife: an unforeseen accident, a slight hitch, a cancellation... what? Why?

Reverend Monsignor Emmanuel Eze sat on what looked like a heavenly throne with his back to the entrance. The groom paused to close the door while Gilbert went round and offered a chummy, traditional handshake routine. Pope John Paul II would object to its practice in church by one of his ministers, unless Francis Cardinal Arinze had briefed him about the harmlessness of the custom. It consists of slapping the backhand three times before the actual handshaking on the fourth swing. Other intricate moves follow, and they vary slightly among different circles of friends.

"Giles, you can't keep people in there for much longer."

"Let them wait, my friend," Gilbert said with a dismissive wave. "Are you worried about power consumption?"

"I understand you brought in a giant generator."

"Brought in? Is that what the Bishop told you? I donated the giant generator to the Brothers of St. Francis of Assisi."

"Oh, thank you... what can I say," the cleric said.

"Oh say nothing, Manny; it is for God's work. Talking of which, where is the Bishop?"

"His Lordship is in the Corpus Christy Sacristy. I am only assisting. School chums apart, I should have kicked against his officiating, considering the cheerless circumstances. I am speaking from purely canonical point of view. I am not just talking about the little problem of protruding stomach, which I am sure the Holy Father will overlook; I am talking about some major issues of Catholic clerical concerns."

"Don't be a dog in the manger, Manny. You cannot teach love and then stop love from flowing on its own steam. Please stop embarrassing the poor boy."

Monsignor Eze looked lazily around and saw the groom. "Young man," he said rather dismissively.

The groom bowed and said softly, "Monsignor."

The young man's mannerism and composure in the face of extreme and hardly hidden hostility impressed Gilbert, but the reverend's stare amused him. He smiled as he recalled the Bishop's reaction when he first broke the news: His Lordship asked St. Paul to show the young man the light before he reached Damascus. Gilbert laughed in his face. He laughed again. It was an inappropriate chuckle, but the bridegroom and the reverend managed to keep straight faces.

"Young man," Gilbert began, borrowing the phrase from the cleric. "This won't take long. I will tell you what you need to know before you marry my mom... Nnénna. If we agree, we shake hands; you breach it, you can forget Judgment Day — that day will be yours. I, Gilbert Chimaobim Iké, will deliver. Manny here, Monsignor Emmanuel Eze, is our witness."

Monsignor Eze looked up, smiled uneasily, and said with open resignation, "Go on, Giles, go."

"He is also an interested party in this little dilemma. He will see that I am playing fair in case it crosses their mind to withdraw my knighthood of Saints Sylvester and Mulumba. You get the picture?"

The groom nodded. His trepidation was too obvious.

"You must be wondering about my fondness for Nnénna. If you have not, please do. Have you ever wondered whether you can compete? Wonder no more; there is no competition. I will tell you a big secret. Do not repeat it; you just have to live with it. Fight it; you lose. I am not trying to be obnoxious; that is unnecessary. I just want to leave my cards on the table. Are you following me?"

He nodded his agreement and swallowed hard.

"Are you okay," Monsignor Eze asked.

"Yes, Monsignor," the bridegroom said.

Gilbert continued: "Here is the gist: My mother slept with my father once, just once—on their wedding day—and the man died. Nine moons later, my folks accused her of sleeping around while in mourning. The man who allegedly poisoned my father championed her persecution. They ostracized her, with a cleansing proviso that the same man offered to bear. She refused. Shamed, she suffered. They did not believe her. Even the church sided with so-called 'practical pagans.' Yes, this same church of Christ...." He paused and pondered.

The cleric coughed, shifted awkwardly, and fiddled with his chaplet. Gilbert looked up. "I'm sorry," he said. It was not clear whether the Monsignor meant he was sorry for what the church did to—or did not do for—Obiagæli Iké, Gilbert's mother, or sorry for distracting his friend's attention.

It did not matter either way. Gilbert thought he wanted to say something relevant and worth hearing. He continued: "My maternal uncles and aunts were her pillars of support, especially Chief Chimaobim Chimé. My own people wanted her out of my old man's compound, but she refused to leave.

She stayed in the house that my Uncle built for her in my father's compound. She suffered so I would not end up losing my paternal inheritance. It was neither money nor land, nothing that my paternal uncles had not shared out amongst themselves. It was about the legality of my existence, my being, my future. Of course, if I were a girl, there would have been no fuss. My mother knew. She felt that I was coming out with the right *particulars*." Gilbert laughed awkwardly. The others did not laugh. He felt the need to explain. "You see, I could have been a great footballer, a soccer star like Pele, but Biafra needed me: I started kicking from the womb."

"Ha ha," Monsignor Eze teased to lighten the situation.

"By the time I came on the eleventh month, she was almost a pariah. Luckily, I came with every fiber from my father. They saw she had a delayed delivery. It was either that or my old man was a holy spirit. Rehabilitated, Mom forgave; but she never forgot. Growing up, I once overheard her praying to Madonna. I still remember her words: 'Aren't you lucky, Mary Mother of Christ,' she would say as she prayed, 'you had Joseph to support you.' It haunted me for years until I became her Joseph. It did not last. She died."

The bridegroom looked up and shook his head, as if to clear his head to take in more information.

Gilbert continued, "Nnénna is my beloved mother taking something symbolic from the Church, something special from the society, something for herself: you, young man."

Monsignor Eze sat up. The revelation astonished him. Gilbert had never told him the story, but what he was saying made sense to him in a flash. He knew of the great attachment between son and mother and between daughter and father. It now made sense: Nnénna is his mother's return.

"She," Gilbert said and paused. He was not sure whether he was talking about his dead mother or his dear daughter. "She deserves justice, even if it is getting away with murder.

So you make your choice: Marry her and come into my family as my son-in-law, my son, her brother, and her best friend, or follow Emmanuel and let her be."

It was a rigid two-way preposition; there was no room for compromise. As confused as the groom was, he knew which way to go. He had decided to go that way, but he did not expect what his presumptive father-in-law was telling him: Why me? Is my life an experiment? Did God design me to accommodate and to accomplish someone else's fantasies? Am I now a little catalyst in life's unseen equations?

He looked up. The stunned stare on Monsignor Eze's face was preoccupied with the socio-religious implications of the disclosure. The groom was worried about his person, not the Church or the society. Gilbert's face was blank.

Just a flash of juvenile indiscretion and his world went weird. The unpleasant ramification of whatever decision he took did not help either. It is just like dealing with a fly that perched on a scrotal bubble. His situation was the sort from which legends materialize.

In his head, he could hear a draft version of pop poem that street dancers must be composing for the next coming-of-age maiden dance. Within weeks, the teenage Erico Angels, the trendy street singing-dancing girls, will shelve the song in the brain of every girl in the city. Before anyone could say, 'Stop it'—especially if someone says so—my whole life will be a song, a sing-along pop poem on the streets.

I, the bridegroom, I will be there with Nnénna, and that is all that matters: She is the salt in my soup, the pepper in my potato porridge, the head that houses my ears and eyes, the meat of the matter, my essence poking pole, the head for which a cap is being sown, and I love her truly.

Nothing else must matter.

Epilogue

HER CHOICE WAS NOT CALCULATED, BUT SHE cherished the outcome. Her life was now a beautiful bowl at which city citizens gazed and construed as they deemed fit. Only marriage will stop the stream of suitors and gag the gaggle of gossipers. Nnénna did it her way. She did not go through university and law school to marry just anyone and make Coal City citizens happy. Outside her executive duties, which now presented no major challenges—thanks to reliable and loyal Lora and other staffers, life was mostly predictable.

Many social friends had moved on; some emigrated to as far away as America and Australia. Her mates were not all married, but she never had much in common with her mates anyway; they no longer challenged her intelligence. Business trips abroad were boring. Foreign partners were now reliable, and communication technology made home-front business easier to telemanage. At times, working from home was much fun, even though it displeased Chināsa.

Nnénna had not seen nor spoken with Zina since she saw her last in London. She had never met her husband Tee Jay. Now Major Dagogo Fynecountry and his wife, Tosina, got their lives together without Nnénna in the middle and still managed to keep each other miserable. Zakky had rolled back his wayward ways with age, but he was still soldiering. There were no real friends in Nnénna's crowded bridal train. Then again, the church wedding was not really about her—she wanted a very simple civil ceremony; it was more about the company, the city, the church, and the community.

As the beautiful bride walked down the aisle, Gilbert piloted her elegantly like the egg of an endangered eagle. Nnénna was happy that almost everyone from her past managed to be in town for the many prep parties and for the wedding proper. The feeling touched something deep in her. She felt as if she was floating away to another planet far removed from Earth, and they came to bid her bon voyage.

The Bishop had put on the last layers of robes in readiness to receive the couple and to commence the conferment of the sacrament of matrimony. His Lordship wore a suitable stole to match his liturgical headdress, a folding cap called miter. His elegant brocade chasuble was immaculate. The pectoral cross and golden crosier complemented his formal vestments.

The moment her father handed her over to the groom, she turned and hugged him most affectionately. Gilbert held her and whispered, "It is well with us."

"To God be the glory," Nnénna responded.

Letting go, she fished out a note from a diamond-studded purse. She gave it to him. Tears blurred his eyes, though he had no clue what it was. He held onto it as he walked to the second right pew and sat beside blissful and chic Chināsa, on whose lips he could read, 'Yes, I now have my husband back.'

The groom was lost in thought as the drama unfolded, a show in which he had a major silent role: Things happened so fast I had no time for creativeness or uniqueness, assuming our conservative Catholicism allows it. Someone told me the other day that marriage does not moderate the trials of life. I know now what he meant to say. I know that nothing in life is going to be easy ever since Satan convinced Eve to give Adam the apple, or so the Bible says. Why he ate the bleeding apple, no one has told me. It is not as if he did not know it was the forbidden fruit. Here I am getting married, and the father of my beautiful bride overloads me with more mysteries and miseries of life. What am I supposed to do at this very point?

In marriage, there are many challenges and temptations... as in celibacy, of course. My singular contention is that I am still at the port of matrimonial arrival, and all of hell's hinges are coming unstuck. Should I advance or should I retreat?

By the time he came back from la-la land, the Bishop was administering the responsive vow. "Do you, Finlay Ezinné Nnénna Iké, take this man to be your lawful, wedded husband, to have and to hold, from this day forward, for better, for worse, for richer, for poorer, in sickness and in health, to love and to cherish, as long as you shall both live?"

"I do," she responded shyly.

"I hereby pronounce you husband and wife in the name of the Father, of the Son, and of the Holy Ghost. What God has put together, let no one put asunder."

The band struck a popular gospel music that brought the church-full of witnesses to their rested feet.

The groom woke up to reality. He could not recall when the Bishop asked whether he wanted to 'take this woman as your lawful, wedded wife'; he did not recall whether the man in question was himself, for the Bishop apparently did not mention his name, nor did he hear his own 'I do' or 'I don't.'

He looked around the humongous church and saw his parents beaming with smiles. He was not sure whether they were happy that they did not spend a dime: the bride being with child postponed the traditional marriage, and Gilbert took care of the church wedding and the London honeymoon. Or, are they truly happy that I have decided to change course, dump a career of circumstance, and marry... just marry?

Shaken with suffocating sense of stupor, he hummed to himself a simple sing-along *rhapoetry* he believed was already in circulation among Erico Angels:

Fada Frank followed family *fa*;
Fada Frank is frankly family *fa*.
Fada Frank fell for Finlay-o;
Fada Frank fathered Fernando.

Frank followed familiar family, forgoing the *fada* family or clerical community—the clergy. He loved Nnénna truly, and he decided to stand by her this time around, especially as she incubated their child. Besides, Frank Obi-Nwaeze is family: Fernando, the ring bearer, is his blood, but only three people in town could claim firm familiarity with the facts. Frank was not one of the three, though he had harbored suspicions from the very first day he set eyes on the boy.

The fragrance of blood, the odor of deoxyribonucleic acid or DNA, is strong and unique. As Igbo ancestors professed: Blood carries the codes of creation and the story of our stellar system; a violation of its sanctity is sacrilege. 'Thou shall not kill' captures the concept, and killing does not just mean homicide. As Gilbert's mother said it to him:

'Do not kill... and I do not mean mere murder... murder is easy; spiritual killing is a sacrilegious stain. Never conspire against any person. Unguarded statements have driven many to early deaths. Whatever happens in life, there is a reason for it; often, it happens to teach you and others a lesson. Nobody is too old to learn. Life is not about what happened; it is about what you do with what happened. You hear what I am saying?'

Gilbert recalled his mother's last words vividly and heard himself ask, "What were you saying?" As folks danced to the altar to wish the couple well and to offload offerings into a central collection container tactically located where the now seated Bishop could see who dropped what, he fished out the note. Exquisitely written in Nnénna's familiar handwriting is an English equivalent of his mother's favorite saying:

> *Even at dusk, curse not the day:*
> *Another day shall surely dawn*
> *As long as the sun will not stray*
> *This new day will be better done.*

Gilbert looked up. Nnénna was looking his way. Their eyes met, sparkled, and smiled. Frank shook his head: There is no competition.

3280825

Made in the USA